Frida Woodard

"Mr. W"

Those Amazing Kids in Mr. W's Class

MIKE WOODARD

ISBN: 978-1-66783-845-8

ISBN eBook: 978-1-66783-846-5

Dedicated to those who are trying to find their place in the world and the teachers who are helping them find it.

CONTENTS

Tag. You're it.

The Incredible Adventure

The five years I spent teaching middle school was an incredible adventure. I met amazing students, exceptional parents, and brilliant coworkers. We shared crazy experiences in a crowded classroom in a medium-sized school in a big city.

The chronology of this book is roughly based on a school year with humorous moments, sensitive insights, and stories of activities and events that will live forever in our memories. However, this book is not categorized by the funny stuff or the sad stuff or the things we learned from each other (many of which have never appeared in a state standard or a lesson plan). The book is more like life itself, bouncing back and forth through moments of laughter, sorrow, silly thoughts, and profound understandings.

If there is a continuum to the book, it is my growth as a teacher. While students were learning from me, I was also learning from them. These complex, young human beings taught me more than I could have learned anywhere else. By connecting with them, I was able to tap into their energy, thoughts, and creativity. It made me a better person.

Let me take you along that journey. I hope you enjoy it as much as I did.

Something Completely Different

… and now for something completely different.

After more than 25 years in the business world, I have decided to give back to society in a bigger way.

I have accepted a position as a 7th and 8th grade teacher. I will teach Career Exploration and Life Skills to middle school students.

I am cutting my paycheck in half for a job I'll enjoy twice as much. Some friends think I am crazy.

It's out of my comfort zone but I am very excited about the opportunity. I know teaching is a humbling experience but after so many years in business, perhaps I need to be humbled.

Prayers and positive thoughts are appreciated.

Tag, You're It

I was hired by Mr. C. He was one of the reasons I took the job as a teacher. I was excited at the prospect of working for him.

Mr. C is the Assistant Principal of the middle school in which I worked. He provides strong support for all of the teachers and encourages high levels of teacher collaboration, student engagement, and student, parent, and teacher empowerment.

He is extremely high-energy. One of his favorite expressions when asked how his day is going is "non-stop."

I constantly see him pointing at people across the room, the field, or the parking lot and yelling "Tag. You're it!" It is a constant reminder of the team effort that is required to achieve success.

His "non-stop" involvement is illustrated in many ways:

- Playing the song of the day as the students enter the campus (usually some type of up-tempo disco or soul song from the 1970s).

- Wearing the tall red and white striped hat from the *Cat in the Hat* during Dr. Seuss week, when middle school students read to the younger students.

- Announcing the Student of the Month from each homeroom at assemblies, telling us what each student did to deserve the Award, and asking them in his best "game show host" voice, "and whooooooooo is your teacher?"

I am always amazed at Mr. C's kind but firm approach to student discipline and his mastery of discussions with parents, explaining the situation and asking them first, "what do *you* think we should do?" It is an empowering approach.

As a teacher, I was the recipient of several classroom observations. Mr. C encourages us to look for new ways to engage students. One time, he recommended showing a video that he had recently viewed that was relevant to the lesson. Another time, he suggested creating six teams and rolling a large die to see which team would answer the next question.

He is always on the sidelines at every sporting event. He has a Star Trek-like ability to "beam over" from the gymnasium to the field and "materialize" back and forth at key moments. I was the coach of the boys' and girls' basketball teams. During one particularly close girls' basketball game, I kept looking over towards him. He was so animated! When one of the girls threw a bad pass, he gave the "no problem, we got this" sign. When one of our girls was called for a foul, he gave the "Home Alone" hands-on-his-face expression. After we won the game by two points, I looked over and he was letting out a low whistle and doing a little victory dance.

Mr. C views the school as an extension of his own family. When I first interviewed with him for a teaching position, he asked me if he could trust me. I thought it was a strange question and I asked him what he meant. "Can I trust you with my family?" he asked," my family of students, teachers and parents and anybody else who is a part of this school?" He must have seen the big smile on my face as I finally understood his question. "Absolutely," I replied.

Then he said, "Tag. You're it!"

Easier Said Than Done

I was in the business world for over 25 years before I became a teacher. I was a manager of market research teams designed to answer key questions for the companies for which I worked. These questions included fundamental challenges such as:

- How do we increase revenues and profitability while also improving customer and employee satisfaction and loyalty?

- How do we best communicate with customers and employees based on what is most important to *them?*

- How should we respond to the biggest threats to our business and industry?

Once I entered an elevator with the head of the Company. He literally asked me for an "elevator speech," a three or four-minute overview of *what's new*. "OK Woodard," he said. "What are people saying about our Company, why are they saying it, and what do I need to do about it?" It was a great question and it was exciting for me to answer.

There was a downside as well. That same individual asked me a few months later to conduct some market research. "This is what I want you to do" he instructed, "and this is what I want the research findings to say." I explained to him that market research wasn't really supposed to work that way.

When I decided to leave the corporate environment and interviewed to become a teacher, I was asked the following question: "How will you deal with students who already think they know everything, may not listen to anything you have to say, and may treat you with very little respect?"

I told them it would be no different than working with executive management in the business world. I would delicately prove to students they still had opportunities to learn things they didn't yet know, we could all have a lot of fun sharing information with each other, we would earn each other's respect over time, and the results would be amazing in the end.

The interviewers must have thought it was a good answer. I was hired shortly after.

Of course, it was easier said than done.

Everyone has a talent or skill, but they may not yet know what it is.

Something For Everybody

Another reason why I accepted the job and was so excited about teaching was the opportunity to teach Career Exploration. I believe so strongly in this class, I think it should be offered at every middle school in the United States.

Here's why:

Some teachers believe that Career Exploration classes take precious time away from core classes such as English, math, science, and social studies. However, Career Exploration actually *adds* relevance to those classes.

Students always ask: "When will I ever use *that*?" Career classes answer that question and add relevance. You will use math or science or English in many of the jobs that you might consider. You might also use your knowledge of history or social studies (what has happened before) as you make an important decision.

Second, that relevance is likely to keep students in school. Make it fun. Teach about a variety of careers. Conduct a project that includes doing something that you would do within that career. See if you like it.

Third, it is extremely important for students to understand their options. If you determine the careers in which you are most interested during middle school, you can develop a plan to learn more in high school. The focus *after* high school should be on some type of secondary education. That may include college, but college is not for everyone. You do not have to go to college to make a good living as an auto mechanic, plumber, welder, crane operator, HVAC technician, carpenter, solar panel installer, and many other jobs. Learning a trade through a trade school or apprenticeship can provide you with a job that is just as lucrative as one you might achieve with a college degree.

The Careers class will not include something the student enjoys every day. Some have no intention of ever becoming a police officer. Others will not want to become an auto mechanic. Still others would never want to become an accountant. You are not going to be interested in everything, but you are bound to be interested in something.

And that is extremely valuable information.

My Niece and Nephew

You will hear a lot more about Careers class over the next few pages but first, I would like to tell you about my niece and nephew. They are my youngest sister's kids, and they provide an example of why Careers classes are so important.

My niece was always good in school. Honor roll. School activities. Very social. There was no question she would go to college. There was no question she would be successful in whatever career she chose. She ultimately graduated with a business degree from a major university and now has a very successful career in Finance.

My nephew didn't particularly care for school. He wasn't interested in his classes. He struggled with his grades. He was on the wrestling team, but he was not going to be a professional wrestler.

Yet, there is something extraordinary about my nephew. He is very mechanically minded. He can take things apart and put them back together quickly. He is a natural when working with a wide variety of tools. He works on cars. He works on trucks. If they aren't running, he gets them running. If they are running, he keeps them running. He is now in charge of servicing an entire fleet of large trucks; maintaining and repairing them and keeping them on the road for a major grocery store chain. He is making great money in his chosen career.

There are many students who get frustrated with school. There are many students who consider dropping out or are very unhappy with the classes they are required to take. A traditional college or university is not for them. My nephew went to a college that focused on diesel mechanics. It was a perfect fit.

Careers class offers something for everyone. We need to be careful about trying to pigeonhole all students into one route to success. We need to present options and ideas.

The fact is that there are many paths to success. My niece and nephew are great examples and they both love what they do.

Careers I Know Something About (and Will Get to Teach)

There are some careers that I was very excited about teaching because I had actually worked in those types of jobs.

As a marketing professional, I played a big role in product development, promotion, advertising campaigns, and measuring product profitability. I had a pretty good idea how I would teach those things, and I knew how I could make them fun (more on that later).

Similarly, I have always been knowledgeable about finance, particularly when it comes to many of the life skills that come with it.

Developing a budget.

Balancing an account.

Taking out a loan and determining the impact of the interest rate.

Understanding short-term and long-term investments.

Sound a little boring? I know how to make it fun.

Careers I know Nothing About (And Still Have to Teach)

I'll be the first to tell you there are other careers in which nobody would want to hire me.

If it doesn't involve a toaster or a microwave, I'm not much of a cook.

My definition of fashion is jeans and a T-shirt.

You would not want me to apply your makeup or cut your hair.

Yet, there are ways of making all these topics fun and give students at least a general idea of what they are about.

So, in my class, we would bake and frost a cake (everybody likes cake, right?).

We would have a fashion show, with name brands and styles that the students themselves wear, complete with a catwalk, music, and light show.

We would have a cosmetology class, giving students the choice to do a make-over or (and this was crazy popular with most of them) apply movie makeup and create a scary monster or character from a horror movie.

That is why it was so exciting to teach a Careers class. For each career, we conduct basic research on the computer:

What does the job or career entail?

How much does it pay?

Where are the jobs located?

Then the students ask themselves a series of questions:

Is it something I might want to do?

Is it something I would like as a job or as a hobby?

That is what a Career Exploration class is all about.

The research part of the class provides context, and the "lab" part of the class provides "practice" in actually doing the job.

With both pieces of information, students can gain a pretty good idea of whether a specific career may be right for them.

The Roller Coaster Ride

First week of school recap: Like life itself, teaching is a roller coaster ride. There were tremendous rewards such as the special needs student who said nothing all day but somehow mustered a smile and a hello to me in the cafeteria. There were engaging discussions with students on the topic of "respect." There was one student who said he couldn't wait to get back to my class next Monday. There were "I didn't know that" and "I never looked at it that way" comments from students eager to learn.

At the same time, 14 different classes with a total of nearly 400 students left me overwhelmed. Some students act out, some with good reasons. Some are starving for any type of attention, even if it is negative. And there is always the one co-worker who tries to make themselves look good by making you look bad. Let's talk about respect, my friend.

Week Two begins tomorrow.

This Class Has a Great Vibe

The Eagle walked into my class, and I was scared to death. I was a deer in the headlights those first two weeks. I was having fun, but I was also completely stressed out.

The Eagle's job was to walk into classrooms and give advice. Some teachers were afraid of The Eagle. He was tall. Imposing. He was very quiet during the beginning of class but would provide a brief, blunt assessment before he left the room. It was nerve-wracking.

The Eagle literally saved my life with three things he said:

"It's counterintuitive but you should teach from the back of the class not the front of the class. That way you can see all of the student's computers and make sure their attention is focused on you or what you want them working on."

"This class has a great vibe to it. It shows that you like the students, that you want to be here, that you know what you're talking about, and you have fun projects for them to complete."

"Relax. Things will never be perfect. There will be some type of new challenge every day. Take a deep breath. Enjoy the job. Establish a rapport with these kids. Trust them and they will trust you. You'll regret it sometimes. Other times, it will be the biggest reward you will ever find. Enjoy it."

From that point on, I stopped looking for "perfect" and began to enjoy the ride.

Used for A Mighty Purpose

Many people have asked me why I became a teacher after 25 years in corporate management.

George Bernard Shaw said it best: "This is the true joy in life, being used for a purpose recognized by yourself as a mighty one…I am of the opinion that my life belongs to the community, and as long as I live, it is my privilege to do for it, whatever I can… Life is no 'brief candle' to me. It is a sort of splendid torch which I have got hold of for a moment, and I want it to burn as brightly as possible before handing it to future generations."

Happy teacher appreciation week to my coworkers, my sisters (who are both teachers), and all teachers, whether in name or spirit. May your splendid torches continue to burn brightly.

Mr. W

Almost everyone in school has a nickname. The teachers are called many things; many of them inappropriate. In class, though, the students need to call the teacher a name that everyone, the students, and the teachers, can agree upon.

My first name is Mike. That won't do. Too informal and too common. My last name is Woodard. That could be appropriate if they stuck with it but they won't. Of course, they'll focus on the Wood part. Everyone does. Woodpecker. Nope, that won't do.

My friends in college called me Woody. Definitely not good for middle school students. Snickering boys and blushing young ladies every time your name is mentioned? Not conducive to a productive class-room atmosphere.

The easiest and most practical solution is to use the first initial of the teacher's last name. As one student walked into the classroom, he said, "What up Mr. W?" It caught on quickly with the other students.

The two syllables of Woodard were condensed to the simple familiarity of W. Already, there is Mr. C and Mr. S and Mrs. G and so on. There is no other Mr. W in the school.

So, there it was. From that point, I was known as Mr. W.

I Want to Be That Guy

During middle school boys' basketball tryouts, one of the players came up to me and said, "Coach, I don't need to be the guy that makes the winning shot. I'd rather be the guy that passes the ball to the open man who makes the winning shot."

Yes. He made the team.

Caring and Compassion Are Alive

In a world of news stories about angry parents at their kids' ballgames and young athletes who care more about personal rather than team glory, it's nice to know that caring and compassion are still alive.

Last night, I picked ten students for a middle school basketball team. Twenty-six students had tried out for the team. Sixteen were cut. It's always a challenge to speak to those who didn't make it. Some were devastated.

I thanked everybody for their effort and hard work, suggested that they "not let the moment define them" and reminded them to never give up. Even Michael Jordan, the greatest basketball player of all time (Sorry, LeBron) was cut from his middle school team.

I knew my words didn't ease the pain for some. One of the students who made the team was going home with his father, when they saw one of the students who was cut from the team walking down the side of the road sobbing. The Dad stopped the car, they got out, and consoled the disappointed young man for several minutes, offering words of empathy, understanding, and encouragement.

The actions of the father and son, reported to me today by a couple of teachers who had driven past the scene, serve to remind me that the negative stories we often see and hear about crazy sports parents and their selfish young prodigy are not the norm.

There are truly wonderful people out there, parents and their children, setting examples for us all.

We're Not Real

I'm at a school open house with a parent and her 7th grade son.

Me: Let me tell you about some of the things we'll do during the school year.

Parent: You don't have to do that.

Me: Why not?

Kid (laughing): We're not real.

Me: What?

Parent: This is a dream. But I think it's commendable that you're thinking about the rest of the school year.

Kid (shaking his head): I think it's sad. You really need to get a life.

Me: (I wake up)

A Highly Relatable Slob

When I worked in the business world, I wore a long-sleeved shirt and tie every single day. Sometimes I added a sport coat. I always had one available in my office if I ever needed to put it on for a meeting or an event.

When I began teaching, I left the sport coat at home, but I still wore the long-sleeved shirt and tie. It was a Careers class. I needed to provide an example of how important it is to dress professionally. And I needed to command respect.

They were *Jerry Garcia* ties: bright, colorful, psychedelic. Garcia was the lead singer of the famous rock band, The Grateful Dead. His ties brought out the inner hippie in me. It was one concession in what was otherwise a very "establishment-like" appearance. That was a problem. A *Jerry Garcia* tie was not going to change a student's impression of a tall, old, gray-haired guy.

I asked my classes about the ties. Some students liked the artsy style. Others didn't like it at all. Ties were for weddings and funerals. I asked if the ties added credibility for me and what I had to say. The students, almost unanimously, said "no."

My wife agreed with them. "Don't wear the tie. They probably think you look like a salesperson who can't be trusted."

As usual, she was right.

I bought a few polo shirts, some with NBA or NFL team logos on them. These immediately brought comments from several of the students. We talked about our favorite sports, favorite teams and favorite players. It was another way to connect with them.

The next question of style was whether the polos should be tucked into the pants or left un-tucked and hanging out over the pants. I am 6 foot 4 inches tall and 225 pounds (at least 20 pounds overweight). A tucked in polo shirt provided some evidence of a protruding belly.

My wife was laughing. "Leave the shirt untucked."

"But won't I look like a slob?"

"A highly-relatable slob," she said.

Teaching is all about the ability to make individual connections with students. The businessman or "establishment" look wasn't going to help me break through the stereotypes and create a stronger bond with the students. The more casual look was a step in the right direction.

Make strong connections with others by listening and learning about them.

The Twins from A Refugee Camp

They spent over a year in a refugee camp in a war-torn middle eastern country. They had relatives who were killed. They had friends who had died. No one else in the school knew what types of horrors had occurred in the war and the camp. The two students never talked about it. Never. And those who knew their history weren't about to ask.

They were twins. She was quiet. A hard worker. Received good grades. Not particularly popular. She kept to herself. But she was a good student and never caused any trouble.

He didn't say much but it seemed that he had a simmering rage burning inside him. He didn't like authority; absolutely hated it when anyone told him what to do. He didn't do his homework. He didn't do much of anything.

He was held back a year, and now that his sister was one grade ahead of him, he had one more thing to rage about. He was fiercely protective of her. When one boy teased her, he attacked him like a lion chasing a deer. He was frequently in trouble for these types of incidents.

They both loved basketball. That was when I realized I might be able to make a difference for them.

When she made the girls' team, she cried. The tears rolled down uncontrollably. I wasn't sure what to do. I found out the tears were not because she was sad. "I've never really been a part of any group," she said happily.

He showed up just as the girls' practice ended. He seemed to lighten up when he was around his sister and took joy in her newfound happiness. There was an hour between the time the girls' practice ended, and when they could be picked up by their mother or older sister.

We started playing games of H-O-R-S-E during that time. He was a master of trick shots. He would shoot high arch shots from behind the basket, bounce the ball on the court from the free throw line and off the backboard and through the net, take shots over his head with his back to the basket, and shoot hook shots from half court. She was more serious; shooting mid-range jump shots, reverse layups, and an occasional three pointer.

I passed the ball to their favorite spots on the basketball court. I never saw them smile so much. I never heard them talk so much. For a time, this was my favorite part of the day. Just shooting hoops with a couple of kids. She won a few games. He won a few games (despite mostly goofing off with his shots). I even won a couple.

Those kids were two of my favorite students. And while I heard other teachers complain about how quiet she was or how defiant he was, I knew different. They were great kids and I had found a way to connect.

Don't Take It Personally

I met a parent after school today. He was walking with his son, looked back at me and said, "Hey son, weren't you just saying how that Careers class really sucks?"

I quickly replied, "No problem. I was just trying to increase the likelihood of him getting a good job in a few years. But he told me he'd rather live at home with his parents for as long as they live."

"Geez, Mr. W," said the dad. "I was just kidding."

I need to take things less personally.

Making The Connection

One of the first projects we did in Careers class was a PowerPoint presentation. The topic was something that every 7th or 8th grade student would have no problem expounding: themselves.

The PowerPoint slides they created (including bullet points and graphics) would provide a visual portrayal of the things that were important to them: family, friends, pets, favorite classes, music, sports, animals, computer games, fictional characters, books, movies, videos, hobbies, and just about anything else they wanted to add.

I gave them a few PowerPoint tips and they jumped into the project with a high level of enthusiasm and creativity. I was particularly excited about this assignment because of the information it would provide about the students.

Students are my customers, and it was important for me to learn about them. By understanding their lives and what was most important to them, I would know my audience much better. I would find the pieces of information that would allow me to find the common ground between student and teacher. I could make a connection!

"You have a collie? I have an Australian Shepherd. Let me show you a picture. You like big dogs? Me too.

"21 Pilots is your favorite band? I saw 21 Pilots at the airport last week!" (Note: It took her a minute to get the joke.)

"You get into fights with your little brother? I have a little brother. We don't always get along, either."

"You like to draw? I'm not very good at that. I can only draw stick figures."

"Fortnite's OK but I prefer Minecraft."

"You like basketball? I know the coach of the school team (It's me!) Who is your favorite NBA player? Steph? I like Giannis Antetokoun-mpo. I'll give you extra credit if you can spell his name!"

"Your family goes to Colorado every summer? Have you ever been to Ouray? That's my favorite vacation spot."

"Your favorite movie is the Avengers? Who is your favorite super-hero? I like Spiderman because he's always on the web!" (Yes, another bad pun!)

"Your favorite book is The Outsiders? Stay golden, Pony Boy!"

The individual dialogue may be slow and awkward. Nevertheless, it gives me a chance to show the student that I genuinely care about them, that we may have more in common than they think, and that developing a connection where we know something about each other and are comfortable communicating with each other can lead to unfiltered honesty and trust.

That's the plan.

Show Some Faith

I took ten students to a Future Business Leaders of America (FBLA) event last week. They were 7th and 8th grade students. I was a little concerned about keeping an eye on them for the Conference and the hockey game that followed.

They proved my lack of faith was unjustified. They took notes on their phones, I-pads, and laptops. They sat in the front row and listened intently. They asked insightful questions. One of them fought through an allergy attack, not wanting to leave. Then they howled like Coyotes, cheering and dancing through the hockey game.

If these students were stocks, I would invest heavily in them. They are truly our future business leaders.

My Middle School History Teacher's Revenge

When I was in 8th grade, I was scolded by my history teacher for talking in class. The topic of the day was the U.S. Constitution and the Bill of Rights. I quickly reminded the teacher of my right to "free speech."

Apparently, I underestimated the responsibilities that went with that right and was immediately sent to the principal's office. My parents were notified of the disruption and were less than sympathetic toward me.

Fast forward to yesterday. This time I am the teacher asking the class to write two paragraphs regarding why they prefer to talk in class than listen to me. One student wrote "what we students have to say is bound to be more important than whatever our teachers have to say." Another wrote "developing our social skills through conversation should be more of a priority than any lesson of the day." Yet another made the First Amendment argument: "First and foremost, it is our constitutional right to speak in class whenever we want."

While I was impressed with the eloquence of their arguments, I set them straight with many of the responsibilities that go along with the right to free speech. I also knew it was karma coming back at me and that somewhere, there was a history teacher laughing.

Extra Credit for Sarcasm

It's almost as if I give extra credit for sarcasm. A group of my students had created a short horror movie. One of the main characters in the film had been injured.

"I can't wake him up," said another character frantically. "He'll be alright," stated the hero reassuringly. "He just thinks he's sleeping through Mr. W's Careers class."

Nice.

De la confusion a la comprehension

I was teaching an online lesson regarding Word documents when I noticed a new student in the back of the classroom struggling with the project. She was visibly upset. When she removed her computer headphones, she looked like she was about to cry.

I walked up to her, knelt next to her chair, and asked if she was having some problems. She nodded. I checked the volume of her computer and asked if she could hear it OK. She said yes, but that she did not understand what they were saying. That's when I remembered she had recently moved to Arizona from Mexico.

She was in a special class and was being taught English by a bilingual teacher. But I was interested in helping her right then and there. I restarted the computer lesson and flipped the audio from English to Spanish. Her sad expression quickly transformed into a big smile. She listened intently, paused for a few seconds, and began typing on the keyboard.

When I graded the project later, I was thrilled that she had earned an A. It warmed my heart that a simple flip of a switch had brought her from confusion to comprehension.

When the Teacher Gets Called to the Principal's Office

Our school has several buildings and a lot of outdoor space. One day as the 7th grade students were returning from recess, one of the guys holding a basketball saw me and shouted, "Hey Mr. W. Catch!"

The throw was too low and reflexively my foot hit the basketball and kicked it way up high in the air. It bounced on the roof of the 7th grade building; once, twice, three times. Then, just as a 7th grade teacher walked out the door of her classroom, it took one more bounce off the roof and fell on the ground right in front of her feet. She jumped back, startled, and gave a little scream. The students laughed and looked in my direction.

I knew what would happen next. It's a little embarrassing when a teacher gets in trouble and is called to the principal's office. But I can't say I didn't deserve it.

Making Learning Fun

Great week teaching the young people.

One class finished their first PowerPoint presentations, creating slides about themselves and their favorite likes (family, friends, pets, classes, music, sports, animals, computer games, fictional characters, hobbies, etc.)

In our ASD (autism spectrum disorder) class, each student said, "three different positive things about three different classmates." We went through the positive things about each student and cheered each one.

In another class, we finished the Technology lesson and played a game I called "Either/Or- Choose One" (for example, LeBron or KD, football or soccer, Biggie or Tupac, cheeseburgers or hot dogs, etc.)

Mr. S and I teamed up for the morning announcements weather report as Johnny and Pony Boy from *The Outsiders* with the worst Jersey accents ever heard (back to youse guys!).

And of course, open gym basketball drills with the 7th and 8th grade gym classes. They're getting better.

I sure hope the students are having as much fun as I am!

Running Through Cobwebs

The assignment was for students to be teachers for a day. They would work in teams to teach the class something and then assign a grade based on how well the class learned.

One team of young ladies found their inspiration on TikTok and decided to teach a dance to the class step-by-step.

They also asked me to participate and I willingly obliged.

However, as I tried to combine the dance steps, I realized the whole class had stopped and was watching me.

"Hah, look at Mr. W."

"He looks like he's running through cobwebs."

"Nice running through cobwebs dance, Mr. W."

They laughed.

They didn't tell me what grade I would have received.

Which One Is Yours?

While at a middle school girls' volleyball tournament this afternoon, one of the moms asked me, "Which one is yours?"

I smiled and replied. "All of them. I'm a teacher."

Try to do what is right, regardless of whether it is what people deserve.

Grace for the Undeserving

My dad has taught me many things. One of them is to do what is right, regardless of whether it is what people deserve.

When I was a smartass, frequently disrespectful college student, my dad got me a summer job at the same place he worked. I would be the first to admit that I wasn't very good at that job. It was technical, mechanical, and I had to use tools that were designed for right-handed people. I am left-handed.

Nevertheless, my dad stood by me and defended me that summer (despite taking considerable heat for his nepotism and the low quality of my work). I did not deserve his support, but I received it anyway.

I continue to see this characteristic in my dad. Kindness is never conditional and the bond between family and friends is always stronger than the behaviors and situations that work to drive us apart.

When my inclination is to be more vengeful and to look for karma to resolve past injustices, I think of the example provided by my own father. Grace for the undeserving. Thanks dad.

The Morning News Team

Every morning, a team of students from my classes would provide the morning news. The broadcast was transmitted via closed-circuit TV sets and linked computers in every classroom on the campus.

We had our own computers for transmission, microphones, and colorful and scenic backgrounds. We had a weather map. We had our broadcasters, camera crew, script writers, teleprompter typists, broadcast transmission specialists, and trouble-shooters.

Every morning, we started with the national anthem and pledge of allegiance. We usually had a guest from the sign language club who would "sign the pledge."

We gave the news, including the lunch menu and upcoming events and activities.

We gave a weather report and sports scores of the games from the previous night.

We provided the Pun of the Day, the Tik Tok Dance of the Day, or "Guess This Song!"

With permission, we mentioned birthdays or special events.

We were scripted but some of our best moments came with spontaneity.

One day, as it rained outside, a cameraman walked up to our weather lady and handed her an umbrella.

Another day, I wore a dreadlocks wig, and together with a student with real dreadlocks sang Bob Marley's *Three Little Birds*. "Don't worry 'bout a t'ing," we chirped. "Cause every little t'ing gonna be alright."

Theme days with Star Wars, Avengers, and Stranger Things characters were common. Funny dances were the norm.

We had our bloopers reel.

An announcer was supposed to say, "big ship" and said "big shit" instead. No 5-second tape delay!

One day the camera caught the weather person crawling on the floor towards the weather map.

Another time, one of our anchors wore a green shirt. With our green screen background, it appeared his head was floating above his body on the live feed.

Once, in the middle of a broadcast, someone pounded loudly on the classroom door. In a loud, deep voice, you could hear me yell, "Come back later!"

We had hundreds of viewers. For information, entertainment, and frequently unintentional comedy, you did not want to miss the morning news!

Priorities Change

For most of my life, I have dreamed of attending the Final Four and NCAA Basketball Championship,

Tonight, with the Game being played just a few miles away, I coached a middle school girls' basketball team.

Priorities change.

More Than "Fine"

Parents. I have an idea. Instead of asking the usual question (how was your day?) and receiving the usual answer (fine), think about asking these types of questions. They are more specific.

What made you laugh today? (Be prepared for a potentially inappropriate response: what is funny to middle school students may not seem funny to their parents.)

Tell me something you know today that you didn't know yesterday.

Give me an example of someone being nice to someone else (including anything you did).

What did the cafeteria serve for lunch today? Did you like it? Who did you sit with at lunch?

What did you do that was creative?

What did you do during recess? Who did you play with?

What did you like most about today?

What did you like least about today?

What made any of your friends smile?

What made any of your friends upset?

What was your favorite class today? Why? What did you do in that class?

If you could change anything about today, what would it be?

What kind of person were you today?

Don't ask all these questions at once. Change them up. Please give it a try and see if it helps open up a stronger dialogue between you and your kids. It may help you get past "fine".

The Day I Completely Lost It

I frequently talk to my students about being accountable for their actions. I remind them that everybody makes mistakes, and we need to "own up to our own mistakes." I talk about the opportunity to always strive to improve and become better human beings.

Unfortunately, I have provided some good examples of making mistakes. One of the worst mistakes I ever made was the day I completely lost it when coaching the girls' basketball team.

Our opponents in that tournament game were an experienced, strong team. They were double teaming (aka "trapping") the ball. We were in our third game of the season, an inexperienced group with great potential, but hadn't practiced how to run an offense against "the trap". After our opponents made three steals and we had two travelling calls made against us, I called time out to regroup.

"Look," I said. "This is a team we can beat, but we're going to have to change our strategy. We know the double team is coming to whoever has the ball, so we are going to have to pass out of it quicker. When you catch the ball, pass it quickly to a teammate before the double team arrives. Everybody else move toward the ball and work to get open. Everybody good?"

"Yes Coach," they all said.

When we inbounded the ball, it came into a young lady who dribbled it twice and stopped.

"Pass the ball," I thought to myself.

No pass. Here comes the double team.

"Pass the ball," I muttered under my breath.

No pass. Now she was stuck in our opponents' double team.

"PASS THE BALL," I screamed.

The entire gymnasium went silent. Not a word. I had completely lost it. It would be difficult to get it back.

I reminded myself this was middle school basketball. Some of the girls had never played any sport before. I had lost my composure in front of them, the opposing team, and everyone in the stands.

The parents were talking amongst themselves. One of them immediately called the Assistant Principal on the phone and demanded that I be replaced as the Coach. One father told one of my teacher friends in the stands he would beat the hell out of me if I ever yelled at his daughter.

There was not much else to do. I knew I had made a mistake. There was no denying it. I had to take accountability for my actions. I apologized to the girls after the game. I called each parent on the phone and apologized to them for my actions. I told them I would set a better example in the future. I apologized to the school administrators in the school office the next day. I promised that I would never again represent the school in such a negative way. I felt absolutely terrible. They all wanted me to continue as the Coach.

Then we practiced how to run an offense against the "trap." We actually became pretty good at it. By mid-season, some of those same girls on our team asked if they could run "the trap" on defense. This time they were the ones who were stealing the ball and disrupting the other team's offense.

From Breakdowns to Breakthroughs

In the cafeteria at school today, one of the young ASD (autism spectrum disorder) students came up to me, and we had a five-minute conversation.

"That was an amazing breakthrough," said one of the teachers. "She never talks to anybody, ever."

I thank God for the opportunity. With this young lady, I am forced to give my full attention, listen carefully, and use more patience.

I pray this will extend to all others in my life.

Learning should be fun.

Marco...

Last week, I received a call from the school office to my classroom, asking for a student. "Marco," I called. "Polo," responded ten students.

Laugh and Learn

Once I was in a class that was being observed by an administrator who wanted to evaluate my teaching style. She arrived a bit late and missed me giving the details of the lesson and the students listening to the directions. The class was already working on the project in groups of four and were quite loud, talking and laughing while completing the assignment.

After class, the observer asked me why I tolerated such behavior.

"They were learning," I said. "I'm not opposed to them having some fun while learning. In fact, I have found they learn better that way."

A few weeks later, I saw that same administrator in the teacher's lounge.

"Mr. W," she said. "I have worked in education for over 30 years, and I have never viewed a class as noisy as yours. I also have never seen a class having as much fun learning. They love being in your class and they love learning what you are teaching them."

She continued. "I have totally changed my view of what classroom learning should look like. I always thought it was laughing *or* learning. Now, I know it can be laughing *and* learning."

Mustard, Pickles, and Tomato

I choose a captain from the boys' basketball team for each game of the season. Tonight's game was three hours away, and I still hadn't picked the captain.

I stopped at a sandwich shop for lunch and ordered a turkey on wheat with mustard, pickles, and tomato.

When I came back to my classroom, I sat down at my desk to eat and considered the candidates for captain. Written on the wrapper of my sandwich was the answer: must pic tom.

That's it! It's an omen! In that instant, I picked Tom as the captain for that night's game.

Tom was delighted. "Thanks Coach," he said. "It's an honor."

I never told him what made me choose him.

The Dead Man in The Courtyard

I finally solved the mystery of the dead man in the school courtyard. A couple of days ago, the 6th graders were having recess in the courtyard and kept talking about a "dead man in the corner of the courtyard."

One of the teachers said, "Dead man? That's crazy talk. There's no dead man in the courtyard." But the students insisted.

I didn't say anything at first but then I realized there was a tree planted in the corner of the courtyard. On the ground next to it was a plaque (looking like a headstone) that stated "dedicated by ..." It looked like a grave.

I could have helped clarify the scene with the students, but I liked their story better.

The Plot Thickens

"Mr. W, you're from a cold part of the country, right?"

"Yes. I'm from Michigan originally. It gets pretty cold there in the winter."

"I have a question. What happens to graves in the cemetery when the ground gets really cold?"

"That's a strange question."

"But what happens?"

"The plot thickens."

Take Time to Understand

The young girl was cutting herself. She blamed herself for her parent's divorce.

The young man grabbed a girl in his class. He had been picked on all day and called "gay" and "fag."

One boy was in a fight with another student. His older brother had beaten him up earlier. His stepdad had beaten his older brother.

One young lady kept falling asleep during school. She had been spending the night in her mother's car. They had been evicted for not paying the rent on their apartment.

It's easy to judge. Take time to understand.

You're Not Losing, You're Learning

I brought the team together after the heartbreaking loss. They looked so disappointed.

"Tough game, right guys?"

"Yes, Coach."

"Losing sucks, doesn't it?"

"Yes, Coach."

"Did you learn something out there today?"

"Yes."

"What did you learn?"

"We need to handle the ball better and not try to dribble out of the double team."

"We need to pass to the open man instead of taking a tough shot."

"We need to block out better on the rebounds."

"I couldn't have said it better. So, we'll do those things better in the next game, right?"

"Right?"

"I can't hear you."

"RIGHT!"

"Basketball is fun, and we learned a lot about ourselves tonight, right?"

"RIGHT!"

"When things go wrong, we can learn from it and make ourselves better, right?"

"RIGHT!"

"You guys are the best. Now put a smile on your face because you make me proud!"

I Would See If I Could Help

The topic was cyberbullying and the question, "If you knew who the bully was, what would you tell them?"

Most students said they would tell them to stop and to quit being so mean.

But one student said, "I would ask the bully if they were OK. Most people aren't naturally mean. They're mean because something is going on, or they're under a lot of pressure, or they're not feeling very good about themselves. I would see if I could help."

Wow. Some days these students just blow me away with their insights!

High Fives and Sanitizer

The story of a middle school teacher. I have never given and received so many high-fives in my life or spent more time washing my hands.

One Too Many

The game had ended over two hours ago. It was a girls' basketball tournament game and it was a Friday night approaching midnight. One of my players was still waiting for her dad to arrive.

I could not leave her alone at the high school.

I could not drive her home by myself. That was a definite no-no.

I could not call her a cab or an Uber.

I could not wait much longer for her dad.

Finally, a car pulled into the parking lot. I walked over to make sure it was the girl's father. I had met him once before. I casually said "hello." He apologized for being late. His daughter got into the car. I could smell the liquor on his breath.

"Are you OK to drive?" I asked.

He seemed offended. "Sure. Why wouldn't I be?"

"Just wanted to make sure. Would you like me to drive you and your daughter home?

He scowled at me. "That won't be necessary."

"OK. Have a good night."

I shook my head as they drove off.

What could I do?

What should I do?

I felt helpless.

I don't know very much about the home life of some of my students. But I do know this: As a teacher, I need to offer whatever stability, security, and safety that I can. I need to be a consistent role model. And I need to realize that while I may not be privy to the challenges they face, I need to show understanding and kindness to them at all times.

Their Favorite Teacher

"You're my favorite Careers class teacher, Mr. W."

"I'm your only Careers class teacher."

"True. But you're the best we got!"

The Magician

Everyone needs a little magic in their lives. Some of mine was recently provided by a young ASD (autism spectrum disorder) student I call The Magician. The Magician's favorite expression is "Ta-dah!" and he excels at making magic out of the mundane.

"Where's your backpack?"

"Ta-dah!"

"Do you have a pencil?"

"Ta-dah!"

"Did you complete your homework?"

"Ta-dah!"

We take so many things for granted. The Magician turned ordinary things into an extraordinary experience. Amazing items seemed to materialize out of thin air.

Everybody needs a little magic in their lives. I saw a lot of magic in a young man I called The Magician.

An Awesome Dog

"What's dyslexia, Mr. W?"

"I'll give you an example: Yesterday in church, there was a dyslexic man standing next to me singing, 'our dog is an awesome dog'."

Stay humble when your life is going well. Show resilience when problems come your way.

I Would Rather Lose with Character Than Win Without It

Is it possible that a coach can be as proud of his team in a loss than in a win? Absolutely! Last week, we came from behind to win a game in double overtime. This week, we lost at the buzzer and I am even prouder. We played a team that won a major tournament earlier in the year and showed how much we have improved since then.

We played a tight defense that held them 13 points below their season average. Most important, we kept our cool while they trash talked the whole game. I would rather lose with character than win without it. I am very proud of our team.

Resting B-Face

The young lady walked into my class with a frown and a scowl.

"Are you OK?" I asked.

"Yes, Mr. W."

"Nothing's wrong? You're scowling."

"I'm fine. That's my resting bitch face."

Stories Waiting to Be Told

Every student has a story waiting to be told. This week, I had a young man show me with Google Maps the small village in eastern Europe where he was born, the airport in Turkey that he flew out of when he was four years old, and his family's final destination of Phoenix, Arizona.

He zoomed in and out of Google Maps with precision and a memorable comment about each place they had stopped.

Every student has a story waiting to be told. All we need to do is listen.

Good Times in Career Exploration Class

I'm having the time of my life teaching a middle school Career Exploration class.

We recently completed a digital photography contest and are currently creating movie characters using cosmetology techniques and movie makeup.

During the next few weeks, we will have the fire department visit. They will bring a fire truck to sit in, equipment to wear, and tools to learn about and practice using (like the jaws of life).

We will fly a drone and create teams to write and record public service announcements. We are also planning a fashion show, will program robotic vehicles, will have a cake decorating contest, conduct a mock crime scene investigation, and design a new website.

Sometimes we will have guest speakers. Other times the students and I will coordinate the discussions based on the information we have gathered. Every lesson will discuss the actual career and conduct some activity related to it.

Sound like fun? It is.

Eating Butterflies

I love teaching because I am always learning too. When asked to name their favorite food, one student wrote "butterflies."

I immediately pictured the student tearing the wings off of butterflies and eating them.

When adding the word "noodles" in the next sentence, I realized they were talking about butterfly pasta.

Today's lesson. Don't jump to conclusions!

Heartbreak Or Happiness?

It was Heartbreak City as the girls' basketball team lost at the buzzer. I was despondent but consoled myself with the fact that the team had little experience and was showing major improvement.

A couple of days later, I continued to agonize over the loss. I was second guessing every substitution, every play called, and every strategic move I made that may have contributed to the loss.

Meanwhile, the girls were talking about how much fun they had, what an exciting game it was, and how happy they were for the girl on the other team who made that incredible last-second shot.

Was it heartbreak or happiness? I really don't understand teenage girls.

Brilliant, Not Lazy

He was a little guy, and he was angry at the world. Lots of fights. Lots of rebellion. He was failing almost every class. He would not read any piece of paper placed in front of him whether it was a study guide or a major test.

He seemed to listen when teachers talked but never wrote anything down. He never said anything in front of the class.

He had glasses he refused to wear. I suspected he had ADD, might be dyslexic, and quite possibly never learned to read. However, he had been thoroughly tested and the Administration reported he was just plain lazy.

He was getting a D in my Career Exploration class halfway through the first grading period. I sat down and talked to him. He said he didn't need his glasses. He said he could read but he just didn't feel like it. He told me grades were not important to him.

On a whim, I pulled a copy of the last written test he had failed. He hadn't written anything on it. I asked him the first question. He responded with an accurate and detailed verbal answer. I asked him the next question. In his response, he repeated nearly word for word the same information I had stated two weeks earlier in class. I asked for verbal examples. He gave them. I asked for verbal clarification. He gave it. I asked for his own verbal analysis regarding the career we were discussing. He was articulate. He knew the material inside and out. He had been absorbing and understanding it, while refusing to read or write one word of it.

During the next few weeks, I gave him verbal tests on new topics, and he provided a spoken mastery of all of them. I mentioned this to his other teachers. Some felt he was just lazy about writing and that I was enabling him. Others said they did not have the time available to give him verbal tests for every single lesson without the "required" documentation of a learning disability. I believe the student is more important than the paperwork.

I ran into his mother who was a volunteer at the High School during one of our basketball tournaments. She thanked me for my efforts but expected he would drop out of school soon. I told her I wasn't as concerned with *how* he communicated his understanding of the material I was teaching; I was more concerned that he could demonstrate a deep *understanding* of it. He was doing that in my class and had raised his grade to a B. She said other teachers weren't quite as flexible and the state standardized tests were coming up and could only be taken as written exams. He dropped out of our school before the end of that school year.

Fast forward four years. He still doesn't learn best by reading and writing but he is studying architecture at a trade school and can visualize and develop the most detailed maps of buildings you can imagine. Quite brilliant and possibly illiterate. Definitely not lazy.

Stay Golden, Doodle Boy

I have a teacher friend with a golden doodle puppy who is also a fan of the book, *The Outsiders*. I overheard her talking to the dog the other day.

"Stay golden, doodle boy," she said.

Don't Worry, It's Fiction

"I'm putting you in my story, Mr. W."

"Is my character good or evil?"

"You're the dad."

"OK, but is the dad good or evil?"

"He's good. You're a fun teacher."

"I might be a better teacher than a dad."

"Don't worry, Mr. W. It's fiction."

The Snapchat Photo

"Hey, Mr. W. Have you seen (xxxxxx's) boobs?"

"What the heck are you talking about?"

"She sent a photo of her boobs out on Snapchat last night."

"She's thirteen years old!"

"We're all thirteen years old. Well, I'm only twelve but ... Have you seen it?"

"Dear God, no. And I never will!"

Apparently, the young lady had sent out a topless photo of herself to her "boyfriend". The boyfriend made a screenshot and sent it to three of his buddies, who sent it to several of their friends, and within a couple of hours, most of the 8th grade class had seen it.

The whole school was talking about it.

The damage was done and could not be reversed. The girl was embarrassed and a week later transferred to another school in a different part of town. The lesson was a hard one.

Students, parents, and teachers need to understand the dangers of social media. Photographs do not disappear from the Internet after being sent out. They can be screenshot and forwarded around the world in a relatively short amount of time. A photograph of a nude 13-year-old is considered child pornography and is against the law to send or receive.

Just as middle school students need to be aware of online child predators who are not who they say they are, students also need to be aware that what they place on social media can have lasting implications on their lives.

Online is forever. You can't control it and you can't make it disappear.

Reuben and Earl

I don't usually mispronounce words or mix them up, but I did the other day.

I was talking about geography and geographic regions, and I meant to say, "urban and rural."

Instead, I said, "Reuben and Earl."

I stopped for a second. The class looked expectantly. And I said, "What I mean is ... Reuben and Earl."

Nobody knew what I was talking about, but they enjoyed my frustration.

Let Them Eat Cake!

I get a stomach-ache just thinking about it.

After discussing culinary careers, food sanitization, and the joy of cooking as a hobby, we topped it off (pun intended) with a project that involved baking and frosting a cake.

Groups of three or four students worked as a team to conduct online research and pick a theme, design, or style for their cake. They were able to choose from a selection of cake mix boxes and baked the cake at someone's home with as many team members present as possible. Then they brought the cake in to Careers class the next day to be frosted. Even in pre-pandemic days, we took extra care to be safe by using gloves, masks, and sanitizer to avoid the spread of germs.

There was vanilla and chocolate frosting, whipped cream, and FunFetti. There were sprinkles, strawberries, blueberries, chocolate chips, Hershey's Kisses, and Kit Kat bars.

With a variety of cake decorating tools, the teams went to work. They had 30 minutes to frost the cake, 10 minutes to eat it, and 10 minutes to clean up afterwards. The designs were very creative and included Harry Potter, Spiderman, Batman, Pac Man, and Jack Skelton (from *The Nightmare Before Christmas)* themes. Other designs included trolls, black cats, zombies, and school spirit.

If anybody wanted to poison me, this was their chance. I was the official taste tester. And just about everybody got an A, even the group that forgot to use eggs when baking their cake.

The final products ranged from great looking to horrible looking, but they all tasted exquisite. From the vanilla cake with green frosting and Oreos, to the chocolate cake with chocolate frosting and marshmallow eyes, to the banana flavored cake with vanilla frosting, strawberries, blueberries and chocolate syrup, the cakes tasted amazing.

We won't get to do this project for a while. We had planned a *Foods of the World* buffet just before the pandemic hit. But this is a great project that can bring families closer. You may want to try it at home. The kids will love it!

Communication, Teamwork, and Collaboration

7th grader: Can I do my presentation on professional skills by myself? I don't want to work with the people on this team.

Teacher: What does your research say are the three most important professional skills?

7th grader: Communication, teamwork, and collaboration.

Teacher: Based on that, what do you think my answer will be?

7th grader: Aw crap, Mr. W. Another professional skill is flexibility. Can't you make an exception?

Teacher: Another professional skill is adaptability. Show me you can do this.

Be yourself, only kinder.

The Best Advice I Have Ever Received

My wife plays a big role in my ability to become a better person. When I am faced with a particularly difficult decision, I always ask for her advice. She is supportive and wise but generally says the same thing.

"Just be yourself," she says. "Only kinder."

One For the Girls

In my Careers class today, students used a kit to build a real working model four-stroke engine.

I had two kits. Five boys and three girls volunteered to work on the project. Each team received a kit. It was the boys against the girls.

After 20 minutes, the boys gave up, but the three girls kept at it. After 45 minutes, the girls made the valves rock, the sparkplugs fire, and the pistons drive the crankshaft.

Great job, girls!!

Global Communication

Watched a team of 7th grade students from Saudi Arabia, Iraq, and Syria give a presentation today on "Professional Skills".

After the presentation, I asked if there were any professional skills that were common in both their old countries and their new one.

One of the students, who speaks virtually no English, came up to me and (with no words) gave me a smile and a strong handshake.

Aren't We All?

Before our girls' basketball win Wednesday night, I mentioned to one of the parents that I felt the team was a "work in progress".

"Aren't we all?" he replied. "Aren't we all?"

You Can't Put a Timeframe on A Masterpiece

Some of my students like to draw, so I decided to have them use a special software program to draw pictures in my Careers class today.

When I told them they had five more minutes to complete their drawings, one young lady chided me.

"C'mon Mr. W, you can't put a timeframe on a masterpiece."

Students With an Autism Spectrum Disorder Make Me A Better Person

I need to be more patient with them. I need to listen very closely and attentively to them. I need to focus on them as if they are the only person that matters at that particular moment.

Shouldn't I do that with everyone?

Students with an autism spectrum disorder make me a better person.

Mr. W-Dude

I love it when students are enthusiastic, but it can become a bit awkward. One 7th grade girl was excited about her *Shark Tank* project.

"I have such a great idea for a product, dude. It's going to be awesome."

To which her friend replied, "Did you just call Mr. W, dude?"

The Dream

Two days after my mother passed away, I had a vivid dream about her. She was sitting in a chair in a large room in heaven. She had an open book in her hands and was reading to a group of young children who were sitting in front of her. Some of them were bald from cancer treatments. Gone too soon. They were all listening attentively.

My mother continued reading to the children, paused for a second, and looked over at me with a smile. I will always remember that smile. My mother loved children.

When I woke up from the dream, I had that same smile. There is joy in working with kids. I guess my mother wanted to remind me.

Etsy, Bitsy Spider

"I ordered something from *Etsy,* Mr. W."

"Was it an Etsy, bitsy spider?"

"It hasn't been delivered yet."

"Did you check by the water-spout?"

"What? You're weird, Mr. W. Very weird."

There are consequences to your decisions. Stop. Think. Consider the possible consequences (both good and bad) before you decide.

Smart-Tough

The kid's dad was furious with me.

"Did you tell my son to be *nice?* Did you tell my son to be *kind?*"

"It was just a suggestion. Getting along with others is important in any career he might consider. Being kind is not a weakness."

"What about standing up for himself? What about finishing it when someone else starts it? I didn't raise no sissies."

"Your son is not a sissy, and I'm not asking him to be one. I'm telling him that kindness is a valuable characteristic, and that it's always important to consider the possible consequences of your actions."

"What if the consequences aren't fair?"

"*Especially* when the consequences aren't fair."

"So, if someone punches him, he shouldn't punch back?"

"I didn't say that. Fighting is an automatic suspension from this school. But he may decide it's worth it. He may decide to teach a bully a lesson. Or he may decide walking away is the best option."

"How the hell could walking away be the best option?"

"We're talking about 8th grade, but what happens now sets the stage for the future. What if he takes a swing at his boss? What if he punches a cop? What if he beats his kid? I don't see anything good coming of that."

"Even if the boss, the cop, and the kid deserve it?"

"Even if the boss or the cop deserve it. The kid never deserves it. Right?"

The man glared at me.

"Right?" I asked again.

"Right," the man sighed. "Mr. W, the world is a tough place. People are mean. People are bad. I want my son to be tough enough to deal with it."

"So do I," I assured him. "I want him to be tough, too. But I want him to be smart tough. I want him to realize that how you react to the situation is more important than the situation itself. You don't bring fists to a knife fight. You don't bring knives to a gun fight. Your son may have to deal with a jerk for a boss. He may have to deal with a cop who has had a bad day. He may have to deal with a disrespectful, rebellious kid. The best way to get even is to find a new job, make sure you don't get arrested, and keep your future open. Kill them with kindness. Kill them with smart tough."

"I think I understand you," said the dad, "but my son better not turn into a sissy ... or a teacher."

For a second, I thought about knocking this smug SOB out of his chair. Then I decided to take my own advice. Stop. Think. Consider the consequences of the action, both good and bad. I would be fired. I might be arrested. I might be prevented from ever teaching again. I decided this jerk dad wasn't worth it. I would be smart tough with him. And kind to his son.

Not Exactly What I Was Looking For

The best not-so-accurate answers to the 7th grade Business and Marketing test:

If another Company has a product similar to yours, what should you do? (*Sue them.*)

How do you calculate profit? (*Using math.*)

Who is your target market? (*It's not a Target market. It's a Walmart market.*)

What is your key selling point? (*Buy this and help me make money.*)

What is an advertising testimonial? (*When advertising finds Jesus.*)

Would You Invest in These Products?

This year's top "Shark Tank" presentations from my 7th grade classes:

Shower In a Can: Take a quick shower anytime and anywhere! A not-so subtle suggestion for the 7th grade boy target market

Primo Flying Hover Board: Fly over the traffic in the drop off and pick up loading zones!

The Clean Your Room Robot: A robot that will clean your room, so you don't have to! Moms like it too!

Healthy Junk Food: Nutritional and surprisingly tasty snacks!

and last but not least…

My Hologram Friend: No hugs and kisses, but there for you if you just want to talk!

Creative new products with strong advertising plans and pricing for sales and profitability.

Please let me know if you would like to invest.

A Wreath of Franklins

"Tell me about your project, the new product you are developing."

"It's really cool, Mr. W. It's a wreath of Franklins."

"Aretha Franklin?"

"What? Who's she?"

"A famous soul singer."

"No man, it's like a wreath. You know, a holiday wreath. And this one has a whole lot of $100 bills all the way around it. It's a wreath of Franklins. Get it?"

"Yes. I get it. It's clever. Do you have the $100 bills?"

"Uh, no. Do you have any we can borrow?"

"I'm afraid not. I'm a little short today."

"Can we use monopoly money?"

"Sure."

"Just so you know. The real product will have $100 bills and it's called a Wreath of Franklins. Do you like it?"

"Absolutely. Respect."

Everyone Contributed!

I am so proud of my basketball team. These 7th and 8th graders won a thrilling double overtime game tonight; overcoming adversity, never giving up, playing with determination, and conducting themselves with good character.

Every player on the team played a positive role in the victory. What a group of great young men!

They're Unique, Not Ugly

Four young ladies asked in class Thursday if they could create a PowerPoint presentation.

They already had a topic and a title: "Don't Judge. Stories About How to Love Unique-Looking Dogs." They didn't want to use the word "ugly." They preferred the word "unique."

Each of the four students found a picture of a dog, gave the dog a name, and created a story about the dog. This was entirely their idea! I can't wait to see the final presentation.

The Balancing Act

Coaching middle school basketball is quite a balancing act.

Would you trade a win by playing your best players the entire game for a loss in which everyone played at least a few minutes?

We lost tonight and some of the parents are very unhappy with me.

The Crash

I was tired. It had been a very long day of school and then basketball practice. On the way home, I stopped at the grocery store (which was very crowded) to pick up some canned food for the holiday food drive.

I approached that intersection carefully. It was always busy and often dangerous. I never saw the SUV. It didn't even slow down as it ran the red light. The SUV hit the passenger side of my car at 45 miles per hour.

My seat belt tightened, keeping me from going through the windshield, but nearly tearing my body in half at the waist. The air bag deployed, hitting with such force as to crack four of my ribs.

I thanked God that neither my wife nor daughter was on the passenger side. I started to lose consciousness...

The Treasure Trove

Sometimes, it is useful to be confronted with your own mortality, to assess what you are doing and where you are, to recognize the blessings you have in family and friends, and the role you play (both positive and negative) in their lives.

Day to day living is fast and furious. It is important to stop and remember all of the wonders (how do my wife and daughter put up with those puns?), the beauty (pick any John Lennon song), and the random happy moments with friends and co-workers that are a treasure trove for which to give many thanks.

Are you OK, Mr. W?

I went back to school before I should have. There was only one week left before the holiday break, and I thought I could make it through five days without collapsing.

My ribs were sore and would remain that way for quite some time. I had a scar on my waist from where the seatbelt tightened. I was walking slowly, looking like Frankenstein's monster.

As class ended, I winced with pain and may have let out a sigh. As the other students gathered their backpacks, a young lady in the second row looked concerned.

"Are you OK, Mr. W?"

I smiled and nodded, impressed with her empathy.

The Luckiest Man in The World

After my recent car accident and broken ribs from a red-light runner, a friend of mine lamented my bad luck.

I responded, "Are you kidding? I have been married to a wonderful, beautiful woman for over 30 years. Our daughter is a brilliant and sensitive young lady. I have a job where I make a difference for many young people. I have caring family, friends, and co-workers.

I'm the luckiest man in the world."

Controlled Anarchy

I have discovered that if I am willing to give up some control over my students and can become comfortable with the anarchy that follows, they are incredibly creative and insightful.

Dad Jokes of the Future

Are the smart-aleck teenage boys of today the dad-joke tellers of the future? Asking for a friend.

Talking Him Off the Ledge

During my first two years of teaching, I shared my classroom with a teacher who worked individually with "troubled" students. She was always gentle, caring, and patient.

One day a frustrated and angry 6th grade boy came into the room. He had been in a fight during recess, was kicked out of class earlier in the day for swearing and was on the verge of a three-day suspension. He was already a week behind in his classes and a suspension would probably result in him having to repeat the 6th grade.

He came into the room, screamed the F-word, kicked a chair, and threw his backpack in the corner. The teacher looked at him and smiled, motioning for him to sit at the table next to her. He sat down and rested his head on the table, facing away from her. She stood up from her chair, moved to the chair on the other side of him, then placed her own head on the table, looking him straight in the eyes.

She spoke to him in a calm, soft voice. I couldn't hear what she was saying.

I had to leave the room for a few minutes but when I returned, I was amazed at what I saw. The student was reading from a book while the teacher encouraged him. That was the beginning of a significant turnaround for the young man.

Had the teacher met his rage with rage, answered his frustration with frustration, and not bothered to speak with him face to face with a soft, caring tone, he would have been suspended and have to repeat 6th grade. Instead, she showed patience and compassion when he needed it most and changed a young life for the better.

Students can sometimes seem like they're standing on a cliff ready to jump. Teachers need to provide that calm, cool voice to talk them off the ledge.

Just Common Sense

One student said the answers to my last quiz were "just a matter of common sense." To which another student responded, "The problem with common sense is that it's not very common."

Good quote from an 8th grader. Voltaire would be proud.

Despite whatever differences we have, we're all human.

We're All Human

Sometimes when teaching, it becomes important to break through biases and smash stereotypes. I have this opportunity when students ask about my own grade school past as a skinny white kid in Lansing, Michigan.

When I was in kindergarten through fifth grade, my family lived on the south side of Lansing. I knew white people, black people, brown people, yellow people -- just about every skin color you could imagine. I knew Mexicans, Puerto Ricans, African Americans, Germans, Italians, Irish, Native Americans -- just about every ethnicity you can think of. I knew Lutherans, Methodists, Baptists, Catholics, Latter Day Saints, Muslims, Hindu, and Buddhists -- a melting pot of different religions. We went to school together. We played together. Sometimes we fought.

"When I went to school," I told my students, "I quickly figured out who I wanted to hang out with and who I wanted to avoid. And it had nothing to do with their skin color, heritage, religion, or how much money they had. "

I relish diversity. There is so much we can learn from different cultures, traditions, and lifestyles.

During the past five years, I have taught students from North America, South America, Africa, Asia, Europe, and the Middle East. I know families that live in everything from million-dollar homes to small, crowded, apartments. I know some boys that act like girls and some girls that act like boys.

These characteristics and behaviors don't matter. We're all living and learning together in a crowded classroom. We don't always understand what the other person is going through. But we listen carefully, find the common ground, and discover that our similarities create a bond much stronger than our differences.

We're all human.

Becoming A Better Person (More or Less)

I will be more encouraging and less sarcastic.

I will be more understanding and less apathetic.

I will be more accepting and less controlling.

I will spend more time listening and less time talking.

Show Faith and Restore Confidence

Two weeks ago, one of the guys on the team I coach had a rough third quarter. He accidentally scored a basket for the other team, dropped a pass out of bounds, had a three-second call against him, and was called for a foul .... all in one minute. I called time out.

"Take me out Coach," he said. "I suck."

"No way," I responded. "In the next five minutes, you'll have a basket, a rebound, a steal, and a block."

I was wrong. He had three baskets, six rebounds, three blocked shots, and a steal.

Show faith when someone is struggling, and it will restore their confidence.

Taking the Bad with the Good

At halftime of last night's middle school basketball game, a young lady came up to me, and thanked me for being her coach three years ago and instilling a love for the game. She told me she was now on her high school Varsity team.

After the game (which the boys' team won to remain undefeated in Conference play), a parent yelled at me for not playing her son during the First Quarter.

I guess you have to take the bad with the good!

Slow Dancing with Edward Scissorhands

I asked my 8th grade students to email me advice I could share with the 7th grade students. The following is an example of what they provided:

"Never slow dance with Edward Scissorhands."

"Don't tell someone the end of a movie if they haven't seen it yet."

"Be nice, especially when you don't want to be."

"Don't run naked through cacti."

"Never kiss after sharing a bag of onion rings."

"Don't eat chili before running a marathon."

"Don't send anything out on social media you wouldn't want your mother to see."

"Expect most 12-year-old boys to act like 8-year-olds"

(From a 12-year-old boy) "You can pick your friends and you can pick your nose, but you can't pick your friend's nose."

Sometimes You Just Have to Take the B

I had a student today who was finishing the grading period one percentage point away from an A. She was missing one assignment that would take her an hour to complete and give her an A. She told me she was tired and would just take the B. I shook my head. What a missed opportunity!

Then I finished the school day, basketball practice, and today's grading. I was going to visit a high school and hear a speaker talk about the potential dangers of social media for middle school students. But I was tired, went home, and watched a basketball game on TV instead. Now I understand her decision. Sometimes you just have to take the B.

These Are Your Major Accomplishments?

Major accomplishments listed by students on their "practice" resumes and my notes regarding those accomplishments:

"I made my bed." (*Just once?)*

"I threw the trash." (*I hope they meant threw out the trash and didn't just throw it*)

"I drowned my sister." (*Did they keep their sister from drowning or did they actually drown her?*)

"I ate three pizzas in one sitting." (*What type of job do you get with that skill? Food critic?*)

"I may win a collage scholarship." (*Without being able to spell college? Or is it a collage for art school?*)

"I passed 7th grade but I'm not sure about 8th grade yet." (*I'm not either*)

Spearmint or Juicy Fruit

The assignment in class was to conduct a mock job interview. I was the employer. Each student was the job applicant. They completed resumes, and we discussed how to give a positive impression when first meeting an employer. Some of the students even dressed up for their interview.

When I called the name of one of the young men, he confidently strode across the room towards my desk. Suddenly, he realized he had a wad of gum in his mouth. He knew he shouldn't chew gum in class, let alone in a job interview. So, he deftly took his right hand, reached into his mouth for the gum, dropped it into a nearby waste basket, and extended that same right hand to greet me with a handshake.

I laughed. "I'm not a germaphobe," I said (this was pre-pandemic). "But I won't shake your hand. Please sit down and answer a few questions." Now the student was unsure of himself, trembling a little, and didn't seem to know what to do with his right hand.

"Thank you for inquiring about the job today," I said. "My first question is this: Do you prefer Spearmint or Juicy Fruit?"

Losing The Game but Winning the Teammate

It was one week ago today. The girls' basketball team I coach was down by eight points with only two minutes to go in a playoff game that would end the season if we lost.

I had a decision to make. Did I hope beyond hope that we would make a comeback and move on to the Final Four? Or did I make a critical substitution, a young lady on the autism spectrum who might be able to finish off her middle school basketball career with one or two baskets?

I'm a competitive coach, but I'm also a teacher of life lessons. I told her teammates to pass the ball and make sure she got a shot near the basket. Nobody else was allowed to shoot. Some of the players didn't like my decision. Nevertheless, they agreed to it.

Over the final two minutes of our season, she took three shots and made two of them. We lost by eight points. But we saw that wonderful smile each time she made a basket. And I can't help but feel we came out winners.

The Empty Desk

I scanned the classroom and stared at an empty desk.

"Where's Jules?" I asked.

"He had to go back to Mexico."

Jules was a kid with an impish grin and a cackling laugh. He was a part of my morning announcement team and a member of Future Business Leaders of America. Jules wanted to be in the United States Air Force.

I taught his sister two years earlier. She wanted to be a nurse in a hospital emergency room.

"Will he come back?" I asked.

"No. Not this time."

I stared at the empty desk and shook my head.

Being Nice Vs. Being Right

During a mock job interview, I asked an 8th grade student "In what area would you most like to improve?"

She replied, "I would like to prioritize being nice over being right."

This is not necessarily an original comment but shows strong self-reflection and insight for a 13-year-old.

A Pun-derful Day

I was pulling a 24-pack of water out of my car in the school parking lot when a young man came up to me.

"Hey Mr. W. Water you doing?"

I smiled. "You're a punny guy," I said.

"I'm a pun-derful guy," he exclaimed.

"My doctor told me I needed surgery because I told so many puns. It's an ap-pun-dectomy."

"You should get a pun-alty for that one."

"Or some other form of pun-ishment."

"As long as you don't pun-ch me."

"I would never do that. They might put me in the pun-itentiary."

"That would be sheer pun-demonium."

"Wow, that's a good one. Have a pun day, my friend."

"I'll have a pun-derful day, Mr. W. A pun-derful day!"

What Does Blatantly Inappropriate Mean?

There are nearly two million jobs in the fashion industry worldwide for adult workers with education and skills. According to *Statistica.com,* the United States alone has over 30,000 fashion designers. The industry continues to grow, and most middle school students have at least a passing interest in fashion.

I am one of the least likely candidates to teach a lesson on fashion. If you're this far in the book, you have already read the section called *A Highly Relatable Slob.* On most school days, I wear a polo shirt and business casual dress pants. On the weekend, I wear a T-shirt and jeans or sweatpants.

In the Career Exploration curriculum, the Fashion lesson involves cutting up garbage bags and designing them into pants or skirts. I had a different idea. That's usually where the trouble begins.

"Why do you wear what you wear?"

"I don't know. I guess I like it."

"But why? Why do you choose one style over another style? Is it expressing something about you?"

"I guess so."

"What do you know about the brands you choose?"

"Not much."

"Then why do you choose them? Is it because of their advertising? Do they have a celebrity spokesperson you admire? Or do you just like them because somebody else you know likes them?"

The students conducted online research in which they learned more about their favorite brands. Where are they based? What range of products and prices do they offer? What does their advertising say?

Who is their spokesperson? What is their worldview? In what does the brand believe?

After the discussion regarding the findings, I told them we were going to have our own fashion show. They could choose the brands and styles.

There was much cheering.

"We'll have a red carpet, light show, and music."

More cheering.

"For one hour, in my class only, the school dress code will not apply."

Loud crazy cheers.

"The two storage rooms can serve as changing areas. One for the young men, one for the young ladies."

"Yaaaayyyyyy. Woo-hooo. This is epic, Mr. W."

Suddenly, I have a bad feeling about this.

"However, to play it safe, your parents must approve what you wear."

"Boooooooooooo."

"You can't wear anything blatantly inappropriate."

There were a few boos but the room went eerily quiet.

"Is that OK?"

"I guess so. What does blatantly mean?"

My bad feeling just got worse.

"How about this? If you wouldn't wear it to the mall, don't wear it here."

"I wear anything I want to the mall."

"That won't work. How about... if you have worn it to school and have not been sent home for it, you're good."

"That sucks, Mr. W. I was sent home by Mr. C for wearing a shirt that said, '*You're killing me, Smalls*'."

"Obviously, Mr. C has not seen *The Sandlot*. Nevertheless, we do not advocate killing, even for someone who thinks Babe Ruth is a candy bar."

I was in a bit of a bind. How do I allow them to express themselves creatively without getting either of us in trouble?

"Look. The goal is to do this without getting you, and without getting me, in trouble. Can we do that?"

"Yes," they responded reluctantly.

They chose from a list of approved brands and a list of approved styles. We had groups wear and discuss brand names such as Nike, American Eagle, Hollister, Urban Outfitters, H&M, and more. Everyone in one group wore Sketchers shoes. One young man was very proud of his GUCCI sunglasses (though it turns out they weren't his). One young lady showed off a stylish ensemble she had purchased for $20 at the Goodwill.

We had styles such as vintage, punk, grunge, preppy, goth, sporty, street, classic, casual, chic, bohemian, exotic, artsy, western, and kawaii (a Japanese style).

We had a red carpet. We had music. We had a light show.

We had no complaints. Not one.

No complaints from teachers.

No complaints from parents.

No complaints from administrators.

No complaints from students.

No student wore anything *blatantly* inappropriate. There was a little testing of the boundaries.

But they all knew what *blatantly* means.

Exhaustion and Persistence

Tough weekend for the girls' basketball team. Due to injuries, illness, and family activities, we could only field five players for back-to-back games tonight. The girls played two 18-minute halves with only a couple timeouts and a two-minute half time break to rest.

Still, they fought hard and never gave up, even though I know they were completely exhausted by the end of the second game.

What persistence! They didn't win the games, but the character and class they showed made me proud.

Encouragement When Needed Most

Another Coach paid a compliment to me during the girls' basketball tournament this weekend.

"I love the way you are constantly encouraging them and teaching them even when they're 20 points behind."

"Isn't that when they need it most?" I replied.

The Truant Babysitter

She missed a lot of school. She was always behind in her classes. Some of the teachers assumed she just stayed home when she wanted and watched TV. Some students said they thought she was partying with high school students. One teacher saw her at the grocery store during lunch.

Her Dad left a couple years ago. Her single mom was working two minimum wage jobs: one day shift, the other, night shift. Mom had no health care benefits. No sick days. No vacation time. No child care services.

So, her daughter oversaw her two younger sisters and one younger brother. The younger brother had asthma and was frequently sick. The others were sick sometimes, too. She was responsible for all three getting dressed, eating breakfast and dinner, and making sure they stayed out of trouble. Her younger sisters were at the bus stop in the morning and came home in the afternoon. Her younger brother was only three years old.

When one of the kids was sick, she would take care of them, staying with them, giving them soup, and sometimes buying over the counter medicine from the grocery store. She wasn't supposed to bother her mother at work. Her mother had enough problems.

She missed a lot of school. She fell behind on her assignments. I set up some time during lunch where she could eat and catch up in my class. Some of the other teachers did the same. A few teachers were not as flexible. They needed time for their own lunches and time away from the classroom. Time away from the students.

She worked hard in my class. She listened carefully during those lunch periods, understood the lessons, and tried to get caught up on her projects. Then she would be gone for the next two days and fall behind again.

I don't have an answer for this challenge. All I can tell you is … it was not her fault. It. Was. Not. Her. Fault.

By The Way, Which One's Pink?

Sometimes I am amazed at my students' understanding of "obscure" cultural references.

Today, a softball player was walking by with a bat hanging out of his backpack. "Be careful with that bat, Eugene" I said. "Shine on, you crazy teacher," he replied.

Multi-generational Pink Floyd fans!!! Yes!!

Good Things Will Happen

Following an 8 p.m. and a 9 p.m. game Friday night and a 7 a.m. game Saturday morning and able to field only a 5-person team with no substitutions and very little rest, the girls' basketball team I coach went into their last tournament game at noon Saturday very tired but optimistic.

"Keep working at it," I told them. "Good things will happen."

Exhausted and acting on instinct, they played a lock-down defense that created multiple steals and fast-break baskets, ran the pick-and-roll, pick-and-pop, drive and dish, and inbounds stack plays to perfection, and came away with a win they may have been too tired to appreciate at the time.

What guts and determination! These girls are the best!

Adding More Detail

Student: Can you look at my report before I turn it in?

Teacher: Sure (Pause). You might want to add more detail.

Student then types the words "more detail" and hits send.

Make The Shot, Turn Around and Say, "Kobe"

Kobe Bryant died today. Some of the kids took it hard.

When my players make a shot in practice, sometimes they turn around, smile, and say, "Kobe".

That's the kind of influence Kobe Bryant had. RIP Kobe.

The Famous Wrapper

In my classroom during a free period today, I was singing songs and putting Christmas paper around several gifts.

One of my students, who was in the room studying, said I was a famous wrapper.

What It's Really All About

I was working with an ASD (autism spectrum disorder) student yesterday. She was struggling with a writing assignment I had given her. I asked her what it was she wanted to communicate.

She slowly and thoughtfully told me this: "A lot of my friends think Christmas is about getting presents. That's not what Christmas is about. Christmas is about family, being with those you love and who love you."

Just Add Another Reference

My 8th grade students are completing practice job applications in which they are expected to provide at least two references. One of my basketball players gave Mr. W and Coach W as his two references. "Isn't that the same person?" I asked.

He had a quick explanation. "Mr. W can say what a good listener and hard worker I am as a student. Coach W can say what a good listener and hard worker I am as a basketball player."

"Listen to this," I answered. "Work hard at adding another reference."

It's a TEAM Game

Parents, really? We win the game by 24 points, and everybody plays significant minutes. We pass the ball, everyone scores, play great defense, and run the fast break to perfection. And you say, "I'm not happy because my son wasn't in the starting lineup." Are you kidding me?

A Very Shady Area

First Aid lesson in Mr. W's class:

Teacher: "If suffering sunstroke, place them in a shady area."

Student: "You mean, like the south side of town?"

Low-Grade Fevers

The topic is health and wellness and how to treat a low-grade fever.

One student said this: "I haven't had a low-grade fever since the last time I looked at my report card and felt a little sick."

Good lord! These kids are too clever for their own good.

For The Love of The Game (And Better Coaching)

I stopped by the high school Tuesday night to watch some of the girls' basketball players I coached back when they were in middle school. There were three players I coached who were on the Freshman team, two on the Junior Varsity, and one on the Varsity.

It was nice to see their continued love for the game and their hard work and success at the next level!

What It Looks Like to Them

During a lesson on improving observational skills, one of my students estimated my weight at 350 pounds. For the record, that is 130 pounds more than actual.

Nevertheless, I am starting my diet today, right after I finish the four boxes of Girl Scout cookies I bought yesterday morning.

Words Are Not Enough

Things are not always as they seem. I saw a student doodling as I was explaining some information to the class today and after I was done, I asked to see the paper.

He had been drawing pictures while I was talking ... and each one was a visual representation of everything I had said!

This is the way he learns. I was so impressed, I asked if I could use it with the rest of the class. I will incorporate visual representations of each new concept with every lesson from now on.

Sometimes, words are not enough.

Who's Columbo?

I went to school dressed as Santa Claus this morning. My disguise didn't fool many of the kids, and they didn't quite understand my generational humor.

"We know it's you Mr. W," they said.

"Really," I replied. "Nice work, Columbo."

"Who's Columbo?" they asked.

The Comeback

Another nail biter. Tonight, we trailed 42-38 with a minute and a half left in the game. I called a time out and told the guys that the game was far from over, but we could not give up another point.

I told them where to position themselves on the defensive end, implored them to move their feet laterally and stay between the offensive player and the basket, and reminded them to keep one arm up and one arm out to defend both the pass and the shot.

We didn't give up another point and came away with a 43-42 win. The guys showed great character and resilience in the comeback. They never gave up, trusted each other, and celebrated in the end.

My Definition of Success

One of my students today said, "Mr. W. You keep asking us in Careers class about our own definition of success. What is *your* definition of success?"

I thought very carefully before responding. "If I can say something in the cafeteria that makes at least one person smile, snort milk out of their nose, or laugh so hard they pee their pants just a little, then my day is a success."

The students gave me a standing ovation.

Choose your friends wisely. Some will pull you up. Others will drag you down.

Three Great Gifts

Over the past two weeks, I had the pleasure of running into three former students, now in high school.

One told me she had never liked sports until playing on the girls' basketball team I coached in middle school. She is now on the Junior Varsity volleyball team at the high school and really enjoying it.

Another is making videos with the High School Media Team after serving on my Morning Announcement Team in middle school. We may someday see her giving the news on a national television network!

Perhaps most rewarding is the story of a young man recruited by a gang over the summer. He remembered when I said in class that "to make good decisions you must be able to tell the difference between those who will build you up and those who will drag you down." He decided to avoid the gang members.

I am so blessed to be given the opportunity to help these wonderful young people.

The Title of Your Autobiography

The assignment was meant to enhance self awareness. Students were asked to create a title for their autobiography. Some of them agreed to share with the class.

There were some great titles:

Fortnite Fun

The Trick-Shot Artist

Amateur Painter

The Mathemagician

The Mean Girl Who Tried to Be Nice

The Kid Who Saved the World

I was quite impressed.

Then the tables turned when a young woman asked, "What is the title of your autobiography, Mr. W?"

"What do *you* think it is?" I asked.

"*Humor As a Defense Mechanism*," she laughed.

The room went silent. She gave a nervous smile and seemed concerned she may have gone too far, saying something she should not have said.

"Perfect," I responded. "Absolutely perfect."

So Dear Reader, what is the title of *your* autobiography?

Call Time Out and Visualize What Happens Next

The other team had just come from behind to tie the score. Our point guard had uncharacteristically missed four straight free throws and looked flustered. I called time out with 38 seconds to go in the game.

"Guys, we've got this," I said. "They'll foul him again and this time he'll make the free throws. Then they will go to their big guy. We'll play a man in front of him and a man behind him with a 2-1-2 zone. Our defense is just too good to let them win this one."

So ... they fouled our guy. He made two free throws. They went to their big guy. We intercepted the pass. Game over.

Whatever challenges you are facing today, call time out. Take a deep breath. Visualize what happens next. Play your game. Be confident. You got this.

I Don't Know, I Wasn't Listening

I was speaking to the school custodian, and he told me a story that deeply concerned me: *Let me digress. Custodian isn't the right word for this guy. He fixes anything that is broken. He keeps the school grounds beautiful, which is a never-ending battle. He even cleans up the barf (both runny and chunky) after students throw up in the classroom and the "Code Brown" situations in the boys' rest room (Trust me. You don't want to know). Anyway, this incredible do-whatever-it-takes Mr. Fix-It told me a story that deeply concerned me.*

"I ran into a young lady in the lunchroom the other day and she asked me if I knew you. When I said yes, she asked me what I thought of you. He seems to be a good guy, I said."

"Thanks, man."

"Well, anyway she says Mr. W told me I would never amount to anything."

"WHAT? Oh, my God. I would NEVER say anything like that to a student. NEVER EVER. Holy crap, what did you do?"

"I said that doesn't sound at all like Mr. W."

"Thanks again. This is terrible. I need to clear this up. Every student has value. How could she think I said something like that?"

"I have no idea."

I thought for a minute.

"OK. Here's what happened. The other day the class was very loud, and I was trying to get their attention. They wanted to keep talking. So, I told them it was a Careers class and if they ever wanted to get a good job and keep it, they would have to learn to listen carefully, pay attention, and follow directions. It would be very important in whatever career they choose."

"That sounds more like you."

A few days later, I ran into the custodian again.

"I talked to that young lady again, and I asked her if you had really said she would never amount to anything."

I had a pained expression on my face. "What did she say?"

"She said you had said something to that effect, but she wasn't sure exactly."

"What did you do?"

"Well, I asked her if you could have been telling the class that listening was important and that if you didn't pay attention, you may not be able to get a job or keep one for very long."

"That's a good paraphrase. What did she say to that?"

"She said she wasn't sure what you said because she wasn't really listening or paying attention."

College for Fido

"Hey, Mr. W. I have a question."

"What is it?"

"It's about education. It's about college."

I was impressed. This 7th grader was already thinking about college.

"Ask me your question."

"If I send my dog to college, will he have a good pet degree?"

The Angelic Piano Player

I always tried to go to the school's choir concerts and talent shows to support both the students and the music teachers. Frequently, I found talents I never knew existed in many of my students. It was another way to find out more about them and things that they loved. These events were well attended by parents and relatives, and I was able to meet and greet several family and extended family members as well.

One night, one of the students surprised us all. He nervously walked up to a large piano and spoke into the microphone beside it. "Hello," he said and the microphone's feedback blared across the room. The student stepped back a little and stuttered with embarrassment.

"I-I-I'm going to perform an original n-n-number that I c-composed last month."

The room was filled with silence.

Then he started playing. I can honestly say that it was the most beautiful music I have ever heard, and I listen to a lot of music. There was a murmur of surprise through the crowd. Jaws dropped open. People smiled and closed their eyes to better feel the sound. The student finished to a rousing standing ovation and stepped away from the piano with a bow.

After the show, everyone wanted to talk to him. "I have never played like that before," he admitted. "It was as if something took over my hands at the piano and helped me touch the keys with a magic touch."

Two weeks later, he was dead. Struck by a car while crossing a busy street.

The entire school was devastated. I was devastated. It hurt. We cried. We felt sad. Nobody will ever forget the young man who played the piano so well that night.

I have imagined him playing the piano in heaven many times since then.

His name was Angel.

Tough Neighborhood

The school where I work is getting a little tough. Saw a 6th grader yesterday with a T-shirt that read "Straight Outta Grade School".

Working Through Adversity

Very proud of our basketball team, tonight. With our best player out with a knee injury, everybody stepped up, passed the ball to the open man, and played a very tough lock-down defense that kept the other team from scoring for almost an entire quarter.

These kids make it fun to coach.

Why I Love My Job

My job is fun. Last Thursday, the coach of the girls' softball team was running behind (yes, we play softball in January in Phoenix). I was on my way to Coach the boys' basketball team but the girls asked me to hit a few balls out to them and I obliged.

I didn't want to hit any line drives and hurt anyone, so I was careful. Too careful at first. I motioned to right field Babe-Ruth style, threw the ball up in the air, swung at it ... and missed!

"Try not to hit it so hard Mr. W," one of them laughed. I followed it up with a fly ball to deep right, centerfield, then left field, and ground balls to first, second, shortstop, and the pitcher, then a bunt to the third baseman who threw to the catcher.

There is something about an aluminum bat hitting a softball on a nice sunny day. It was exhilarating and the smiles on the girls' faces made it all the more rewarding.

The fact that I have these moments as part of my job is simply amazing. I love it.

Pressure? What Pressure?

We had two must-win games over the weekend. We won both and it's on to the Final Four semifinal game Wednesday night. Win that and it's on to the Championship Game Friday.

When we got to the semifinal game, the team seemed jittery.

"Look guys," I said. "We all know it's a big game. It would be nice to win this one and play for the Championship. We've practiced all season for this. More important, though, I just want you to go out and have fun. Let's play the game because we enjoy it and we enjoy being with each other. OK?"

We had more more fun in that game than we had in any game all season. And we lost. By one point. There were no tears. Only smiles.

Our season was over. But what a season. We lost our first game and lost our last game of the season. In between, we won 11 straight games. We made unbreakable friendships along the way. We learned the meaning of teamwork. We became a very good team.

Not a Championship team. But none of us would have traded it for the world.

As I told one of the players going into that final game, "Relax. Don't feel the pressure." He smiled back at me and said, "Pressure? What pressure?"

When Life Doesn't Go Your Way

With tonight's loss, our team finished the season short of our goal of winning a championship. Nevertheless, we learned much about the game of basketball and each other.

I have always felt that it is losing, not winning, that defines character. When you are winning (like during that eleven-game win streak) and everything is going your way, life is easy, and the world is your oyster. You try to stay humble, but it's hard.

How you react to losing is what really matters. Can you lose with grace? How do you react when things do not go the way you want or expect? That is the real lesson and there is the real learning. Can you use those experiences to make yourself a better person? I believe you can.

Teaching the intricacies of a sport is important, but the greatest knowledge a coach can share is how to win with humility and how to lose with grace.

I thank those 12 young men for sharing the experience of a basketball season and becoming a "family" of teammates with their coach. It was an honor and a privilege.

We Are All On the "Spectrum"

About a month ago, the basketball team I coach was playing another team, and we were winning handily. However, there was a kid on the other team who was playing his heart out, diving for loose balls, scrambling for rebounds, passing to teammates, and making a few tough shots. I was impressed and sought him out after the game.

The coach of their team said, "Oh, that kid? He's a little weird. He's over there in the corner crying (about the loss)."

I went over and shook the boys' hand and told him he had played a great game. His mother was with him. When he didn't say anything back to me, she said apologetically, "He's still upset. He's on the spectrum, as they say." "Aren't we all?" I replied, smiled, and held out my hand to her. She began to cry. I can barely comprehend the struggles she has known. But all I saw was a kid who played a great basketball game, and a loving mother standing by his side.

My comment was sincere. We all have nuances, challenges, unique habits, and awkward ways of expression. We are all on this "spectrum" and we should respect all others on it as well.

Middle School Rhapsody

I was asked to sub the last 15 minutes of choir class yesterday. I have no background in teaching choir but I took the opportunity to teach *Bohemian Rhapsody* (with a few lyric changes).

These included my solo: "I'm just a poor teacher. Nobody loves me."

And their verse, "Mama, just got an F. Didn't study for my test. Woe is me. Now I'm stressed."

I have a feeling I won't be asked to teach choir again anytime soon.

If You Can Solve Problems, You Will Succeed in Life

Very proud of my *Future Business Leaders of America* team! Several students participated in today's Regional Competition and all of them had a great experience. Three students took 1st place in the Critical Thinking (Problem Solving) category. One took 3rd place in Business Etiquette. Another took 3rd place in Computer Programming and Coding.

We have placed a lot of emphasis in my class on critical thinking and problem solving as it relates to life and future employment opportunities. Whether it's trying to deal with life's many challenges or a specific issue at school or work, the ability to come up with potential solutions and probable consequences for each is critical to success.

Blessed

I usually speak well of my students, but I don't want you to think educating young people is always a joy.

There was the student who knocked on the classroom door and then pretended he was hit in the head when I opened it. There was the chewed gum on my chair that I noticed just before I sat down. There was the missed high five that resulted in a slap on my nose.

Ah yes, teaching. I am so blessed.

The Best Thing That Ever Happened

I have a friend who is a boys' basketball coach at another middle school in the district. We beat them by three points earlier in the year. Tonight, his team won the Championship. I spoke with him after the game.

"That loss to your team was the best thing that ever happened to us," he told me. "My guys were much more focused after that. They realized they still had to work hard and improve. Thank you for helping us win this Championship!"

The Case of The Stolen Backpack

We had just finished a lesson the day before regarding safety in the workplace and I wanted to dig a little deeper into the subject of *situational awareness*.

As the class began, the students came in, sat down, and continued talking to each other. They knew that the first words I said would command their attention. What they didn't know was that I had something different planned for them on this day.

I was carrying a backpack at my side. While I looked out at the class, they continued chatting, oblivious to what would happen next. From the corner of the room, a young man wearing a mask ran up to me, knocked me off balance, grabbed the backpack and ran out the door.

"Wait. What just happened?"

"What the heck?"

"Oh my God."

"Mr. W. Are you OK?"

"I'm fine," I replied. "That whole incident was staged. Today's lesson is about situational awareness, and the importance of always being aware of your surroundings and what is happening around you. Now, tell me what you just saw."

Some students didn't see anything. They were busy talking to each other and had no idea what was going on. Other students gave a description of the assailant, but the descriptions varied. They argued with each other. Was he tall or short? What was he wearing? What color was the mask? What type of shoes did he have? Eventually, they came up with a description of which they were very confident.

I brought the person who "stole the backpack" back into the classroom. He still had the mask on. The description from the students had not been very accurate.

I followed this up with a video. "As you can tell, a lack of awareness can create inaccurate descriptions of an incident. However, focusing too much on one thing and not on the big picture can also make you miss something important."

In the video, a group of young men and women were in a circle and passing or bouncing a basketball to each other. The task for my students was to count the number of passes during the short video. There was a consensus about the number of passes that were made.

"I'm impressed. You're right about the number of passes. How many gorillas were in the video?"

"What?"

"You're messing with us, Mr. W."

"There weren't any gorillas in the video!"

I played the same video again. As our eyes were trained on the movement of the ball, a man in a gorilla costume walked through the middle of the circle and then walked away. Most of the students had missed it the first time.

"How did we miss that?"

"I didn't even see it!"

"I was watching the basketball."

The lesson was clear. First, the students had missed the person knocking me down and then they missed the gorilla in the video.

We discussed situational awareness and how and why it was important. I discussed my traffic accident from earlier in the year. One person tearfully mentioned Angel. We talked about avoidable accidents on the playground. We discussed witnessing a crime and talking to the police. We discussed how looking at our phones all the time reduced our situational awareness.

Some of the student-athletes talked about the need to focus during their volleyball, football, basketball, and softball games. It meant not just keeping their eyes on the ball but knowing how the other team was positioned whether on offense or defense. It meant knowing what your teammates were doing. It meant paying attention even if you were on the bench, since you might enter the game at any given moment.

It was a good discussion and the students vowed they would pay better attention to their surroundings. I continued to test their awareness several times over the next few weeks. I hoped they would not forget what they learned. This was a lesson that could make a big difference in their lives.

Two months later, one my students and his mother visited me in my classroom before school. They were both excited to tell me a story about what had happened on their way home from school the previous afternoon.

"I picked him up at the usual time and we were driving home," the mother began.

The son jumped into the conversation. "Mr. W, I never used to pay any attention at all on the drive home, but since that situational awareness class, I've been looking around more. I watch the people on the sidewalks, in the other cars around us, and wave to my friends who are walking home."

"This truck was coming out of the grocery store. It didn't even stop. It turned right in front of us. I said, 'Mom, look out!'

I never would have seen it," admitted the mom. She looked over at her son. "If he hadn't warned me, I wouldn't have stopped in time, and that truck would have hit the side of our SUV. The driver was going too fast. It would have caused some damage and we could have been hurt."

"Thank you, Mr. W. We have first-hand experience in the importance of situational awareness, and we want to thank you for teaching it during your class."

They had brought me a dozen donuts in appreciation.

Luckily, I had situational awareness of how much weight I had gained during the previous month. I ate one donut to show my gratitude and took the rest to the teacher's lounge.

The True Value of Basketball

I was talking to a parent tonight after our basketball game. She said, "I know you're trying to teach basketball, but I don't care about that. I care that my daughter understands that success as a team is better than individual glory, that practice and hard work will make you better, and that those less fortunate or talented should be given a chance." I am blessed with the opportunity to teach those values through the game of basketball.

There are many paths to success.

A Brand-New World

Awareness of the pandemic came in the middle of a girls' basketball tournament. They shut down the tournament and closed the schools. The night before, I had high-fived over 40 young ladies, including our team and two teams we had played against.

Of course, I was concerned. My top priority was the safety of the students and their own mental health and physical well being. We were in uncharted territory.

Spring break came and went, and we began teaching students remotely. We gave out laptops. Most students had internet access from their homes. They could login through Microsoft Teams and participate in a virtual class. It was different than being in a classroom. I had them keep their cameras on so I would know they were paying attention. They could communicate by chat or by turning their microphones on when I asked them a question or when they had a question for me.

I tried to continue making Careers class fun. We started with the "bad joke of the day". It was usually some type of cheesy Dad joke, but eventually the kids started telling jokes of their own, some appropriate, others not so much. I could still show them videos regarding various careers. I could also show them funny videos to lighten things up a little.

We could still conduct research online regarding job descriptions, salaries, education requirements, and where the largest number of these jobs were located. We had continued access to computer games that focused on careers such as computer programming, architecture, interior design, and more. Email and chat became the primary modes of communication.

The pandemic closed some doors as far as in-class activities, but it opened several other doors with virtual at-home learning opportunities. There were a variety of educational activities that had been made available for **free** from several organizations and businesses. The students were able to learn and see things they might never otherwise have experienced. These included:

- 38 virtual 360-degree National Park tours

- 20 virtual field trips to take with kids

- 18 best podcasts for middle school students

- 18 educational games and activities for kids (Ask Alexa)

- 300,000 books to download from the New York Public Library

- Virtual rides at Disney parks (not recommended after lunch)

- NASA media library and STEM activities

Once a week, we participated in some type of virtual "field trip". As a class, we went to the San Diego Zoo and Yellowstone National Park.

We watched "live" video from NASA of the Mars land rover. We took a virtual trip to a zoo where the animals were wearing cameras and saw life at the zoo from the animals' perspective. We spent a morning on a farm by video, witnessing "live" a day in the life of a farm family.

We could communicate back and forth and my "city kids" had a lot of questions.

I made sure we stood up and exercised after the first 20 minutes of every class. I gave the students time to stand and stretch and talk to each other online for a few minutes. It was a challenge sometimes to reel them back in, but I didn't want them sitting, staring at a computer for an hour without any physical activity or socializing.

Some students did not have internet access. I spoke to those students individually by telephone and gave them abbreviated lessons, asking them questions at the end of the call to determine levels of understanding. I made daily calls to over 30 students. I needed to keep them engaged. I did not want them to fall through the cracks.

It was a big adjustment for all of us. I wasn't as concerned that we make it through the curriculum as I was that we all stayed healthy, both physically and mentally. Parents were losing jobs. People were getting sick and dying. The virus became a political issue. Students were caught in the middle of all of it.

Once again, I was trying to offer stability, security, and reassurance. It was tough. Some didn't show up for their online classes. They were working at their parents' small businesses to try to keep them afloat. Some families moved in with relatives because they couldn't pay their mortgages.

Yet, most of them persisted. Students are more resilient than we think. They are generally more adaptable than adults.

In a worldwide crisis, they were doing quite well.

I knew that at some point, we would return to school and in-class teaching. It was inevitable. And that would create an even bigger challenge for me.

The Family Store

The pandemic brought new challenges to many students. Some did not have internet service at their homes or apartments. They completed their lessons the old-fashioned way: on paper. They picked up paper packets at the school, or we dropped them off at their homes. We talked to them on the telephone and made sure they understood their assignments. They dropped off their completed work at the school or we picked them up at their homes. If that sounds like a lot of extra work for teachers, it is.

One young lady in 8th grade had a unique challenge. She was not completing her assignments even though she had a computer and internet service. She was two weeks behind when I called her parent's phone number. She answered the phone.

"Hey Mr. W. How are you?"

"I'm good. How have you been?"

"I'm very busy. I have been working at my parents' store."

Her parents had a small store that sold Middle Eastern food and specialty items.

"What have you been doing at the store?" I asked.

"I use my phone to contact customers we haven't seen in a while, ask them if I can order something for them, take it directly to their address, and collect the payment. My parents say it is the only way to keep our store open."

"Sounds like you're putting what you learned in Future Business Leaders of America to good use. I can give you some extra credit for that. What about the homework from your other classes? I know you are falling behind."

"I'm sorry, Mr. W. I can't do that right now."

"The law says you are supposed to be going to school online."

"I know."

"If you fail these classes, you will need to repeat 8th grade next year."

"That's OK. My family needs me right now. If we have to close the store, we can't pay for our food and rent. We may have to go back to Afghanistan. We don't want to do that. It's not safe. I would rather repeat 8th grade. Family comes first. You know that, right?"

"Yes, I do. Promise me you will come back to school when you can."

"I promise."

"Is there anything I can do to help?"

There was a short pause. "Would you buy some Torshi?"

MC Macaroni

I wanted to do something fun online for the students, so we decided to play a name game. There are a lot of similar name games online (some inappropriate for students). In this one, everyone has six names. You can play along.

1. Your actual name

2. Your TV character name (middle name plus name of street where you live).

3. Your Star Trek name (first three letters of last name, first two letters of middle name, last two letters of first name)

4. Your superhero name (color of shirt and that thing on your left)

5. Your Goth band name (Black and the name of one of your pets)

6. Your rap-star name (MC and the last thing you ate)

When the Teacher Becomes the Student

There are so many things I learned from my students. There are times when it seemed like they were the teachers, and I was the student. These are a few of the most important things I learned (and they apply not just in the classroom but in the workplace and life in general).

- *Students are amazing, creative, funny, and complicated.* I guess I took that for granted but actually seeing it on a daily basis is incredible. Their creativity is only limited by the restrictions we place on them. Their humor may sometimes sound crude but is just as often clever. They are not simple and easy to understand. They are complicated, just like older people. They are juggling a variety of challenges simultaneously and trying hard to make sense of the world around them. They are amazing in so many ways.

- *Problems are not always what they seem.* Remember the story of the truant babysitter? She wasn't skipping school! Remember the story of the kid who was doodling during class? He was paying attention the whole time and taking notes in the way that was most helpful to him. Don't assume negative intentions or non-existent motives. You may miss the mark and make the situation worse.

- *Stop talking and listen carefully.* Have you ever been in a class where the teacher talked for an hour and then the class was over? That is not teaching! Teaching is two-way communication. In the musical *Hamilton*, Aaron Burr gives Alexander Hamilton advice that may apply to many teachers. Talk less. Smile more.

Over time, I learned to listen carefully to my students. Some of them did not initially trust me. Some did not want to talk to me. Sometimes the language was non-verbal, and I had to observe it. Occasionally, the language was not very complimentary toward me. I listened and tried very hard to appreciate their viewpoints.

- *Take the time to really understand.* More than anything, what students need is your time (and teachers, of course, have very little time to spare). What happens when a teacher tells a student they have no time for them? What does that do to create trust? What does that do to the student's self-esteem? What does that do to solve a problem or create an understanding of an assignment that is due the very next day. Take a deep breath. Take the time. It will be worth it.

- *You may never know about their home life challenges.* Does Dad have one too many? Is mom verbally abusive? Is the older brother a bully? Are mom and dad always fighting and about to get a divorce? Is *nana* sick and about to die? Are they one bill away from being homeless? Do they have to wear hand-me-downs because they can't afford new clothes? Or are they living in a million-dollar home where material possessions take priority over actual human beings, and work seems more important than quality family time? You may not know anything about their life outside of school. Offer stability when there is none anywhere else. Tell them you care when they may not hear it from anyone else. Give them the benefit of the doubt when they are doubting themselves.

- *Teach by example.* Set the example you want them to be, while understanding that they may not achieve these goals right now. You want them to act kinder? Show them kindness. You want them to act patiently? Show them patience. You want them to stop being so cliquish? Stop trying to hang out with just the cool teachers. You want them to use more appropriate language?

How do you speak when you think no one is listening? Every teacher makes mistakes. Hold yourself accountable when you make mistakes. Admit it when you are wrong. Say you are sorry and will try to do better. Students will respect you and remember you for it.

The Most Personally Rewarding Job I Have Ever Had

Thus ends the teaching career of "Mr. W." What a wonderful experience. It was the most personally rewarding job I have ever had. The ability to teach a relevant and fun curriculum, and coach both boys' and girls' basketball teams, was a dream come true.

However, when forced to choose between a job I love and the health and safety of my immune-compromised wife of 35 years (that is, we have been married 35 years, she is not 35 years old), I will choose my wonderful wife EVERY SINGLE TIME. I love my job, but I can live without it. I can't live without my wife. I love her more than anything.

My thanks to the head of the Career Exploration Department at the district and the principal and assistant principal at the school for making my dream of teaching a reality. My thanks to my co-teachers in the Career Exploration Curriculum for providing tips to help make it the most fun, relevant, and useful curriculum I have ever seen.

My thanks to those teachers who provided great examples of classroom teaching, showed how to best motivate, explained when to push and when to hold back, and that you should always listen first. "Are you OK?" should be your first question, not, "Why didn't you turn in your homework?"

I learned so much from so many and that includes all that I learned from my students. I learned as much, if not more, from them as they learned from me.

I was truly blessed by my teaching experience. And I am truly blessed by whatever comes next.

Four Hours of Fortnite

Anybody who says a kid can't learn virtually and must have face to face socializing every day has never seen them play online with their peers all in different locations for four straight hours.

A Noble Thing to Do

When the students found out I was not going to be their teacher any more, some were upset, and some were indifferent.

One student, who realized I was quitting mostly to protect my wife from sickness, was very pragmatic about it.

"I understand completely Mr. W," he said. "That is a noble reason, and you, sir, are a noble man."

Rascals and Reptilians

"You know, not everyone is sad to see you go, Mr. W."

"Really. Why not?"

"Well, not everyone likes you."

"Really? Why don't they like me?"

"Because they are rascals and reptilians."

"Rascals and reptilians?"

"Yes. Rascals who don't pay attention, don't do their homework, and always get into trouble."

"And reptilians?"

"Yes. They are cold, Mr. W. Cold, clammy creatures. Like reptiles."

"Well, I like rascals and reptilians," I replied. " I'm sorry they don't like me."

The Last Class

On the last day I taught middle school, I had three pieces of advice for my classes. I told them that if they did not remember anything else that I had ever taught them, I would like them to remember these three things:

1. Choose your friends wisely.

Your friends can either make you or break you. Some friends will lift you up when you are down, support you when others "throw shade," and let you know when you are screwing up and need to be straightened out a little. Other "friends" will lead you down dangerous paths, abandon you to save themselves, and prove they can't be trusted. Some friends will lift you up. Others will pull you down. And it's critical to know which friend is which.

2. Make good decisions.

Everybody makes mistakes. But one of the ways to make fewer mistakes is to think first about the consequences of your actions. What happens if I skip this class? What happens if I don't do my homework? What happens if I don't study for this test? What happens if I smoke this joint or drink this beer? What happens if I place this photo on social media?

What are the pros and cons of the decisions I make? What good may come of it? What bad may come of it? If you stop and think for a minute, you may realize that the potential consequences of a certain action are not worth it. It can make a difference in your future; short term and possibly long term.

3. There is a job out there for you.

Middle school is not too early to start thinking about the things you might like to do for a career and, just as important, the things you don't want to do for a career. Everybody has a talent. Everybody has something they enjoy. Can you get paid doing that? Can you make it a career of some type? Should you cultivate that skill? Maybe it becomes a hobby while you get paid to do something else that pays the bills. There's nothing wrong with that. But if it's legal, and you like doing it, don't let it go.

Everybody has a talent. Sometimes these talents are hidden. Try to find your talent. Try to find your passion. Try to find what you like to do most and then use it to enjoy every day of your life.

Try to remember these three things:

- Choose your friends wisely.

- Make good decisions.

- There is a job out there for you.

They'll Be Fine Without Me

After telling my students that I was going to quit teaching and they would have a new teacher soon, some of them were very concerned.

"Will she tell us the bad joke of the day?" one of them asked.

"I don't know," I replied. "That's up to her."

"Maybe she'll tell us the good joke of the day instead of the bad joke," another one said.

"Ouch," I thought. Then I smiled. Because I knew. The students would be just fine without me.

Peas, Puns, and Amazing Kids

Every holiday season, during the canned food drive, I purchased (among other things) a can of peas and a can of hominy. Somehow, during the last canned food drive, these two cans were never picked up. So, I left them on my desk in my classroom.

When I left school due to the pandemic, I dropped the peas and hominy off with Mr. C, the assistant principal. When I talked to him and a few teachers several weeks later, I found out that the peas and hominy were being sent to a different classroom at the end of each day.

"Who needs a little peas and hominy?" was the running joke.

Peas and hominy. Peace and harmony.

Mr. C said it was an example of my legacy at the school.

"What legacy is that?" I asked.

"Bad puns and good intentions."

"Thank you, Mr. C. That's very kind. But it's not really about me."

"It's not? What's it about?"

"It's about those kids, Mr. C. *Those amazing kids in Mr. W's class.*"

Final Exam 1

Write down the item that you need to remember the most.

- Everyone has a talent or skill, but they may not yet know what it is.

- Make strong connections with others by listening and learning about them.

- Try to do what is right regardless of whether it is what people deserve.

- Learning should be fun.

- Stay humble when your life is going well. Show resilience when problems come your way.

- Be yourself, only kinder.

- There are consequences to your decisions. Stop. Think. Consider the possible consequences (both good and bad) before you decide.

- Despite whatever differences we have, we're all human.

- Choose your friends wisely. Some will pull you up. Others will drag you down.

- There are many paths to success.

Final Exam 2

Please consider the following items that I learned when working with students (This may also apply to coworkers or other people in your life).

- They are amazing, creative, funny, and complicated.

- Their problems are not always what they seem.

- Stop talking and listen carefully to them.

- Take the time to really understand them.

- You may never know about their home life challenges.

- Be the example you want them to be.

In Gratitude

Special thanks to my wife and daughter, my mother and father, and my sisters (who are both teachers). I am forever indebted to my coworkers in the business world who became great friends and those few brave souls who waded through early drafts of this book.

Thank you to the people who put their faith in me by hiring me as a teacher, the parents who provided advice, support, and insights into their kids, and the teachers who modeled the best ways to enjoy both the most challenging and most rewarding job in the world.

Most of all, my gratitude goes out to those amazing, creative, funny, and complicated students who made it an honor and a privilege to teach them and who taught me many incredibly valuable life lessons.

Finally, my thanks to the publisher for making this book possible and the readers for giving it a chance. I pray it is helpful.

About The Author

Mike Woodard is a graduate of Michigan State University and worked for over 20 years as a Market Insights Director for large corporations. Then he found his dream job as a middle school teacher.

He taught Career Exploration classes and coached both the boys' and the girls' basketball teams. It was an eye-opening experience. Sometimes the roles would reverse. The teacher became the student, and the students became the teacher.

Woodard is currently retired from teaching and lives with his wife in Glendale, Arizona, where he continues to play basketball, moderate online discussion groups, and listen to a wide, eclectic mix of music.